All That Comes After

THE HERE WE REMAIN SERIES BOOK II

WRITTEN BY: M. HOMES

ILLUSTRATION BY: JESS REESE

EDITOR: SUSAN CHASE

Chapter:1 Beer Run

November 13, 2013

Chris, Sarge, and Mark are having a meeting about supplies in the back bedroom of the cabin Mark had once used to grow unlawful plants. It has its own electrical wind power. The bedroom's the biggest room out of the three. It has a big window that looks out on the once pretty field that is now starting to grow back after the firebombing last summer. Having been in the cabin for months, supplies and patience, are running low. Mark's face is still clean shaven with the same fullness it had back when all of this started, but his hair is getting shaggy now. He doesn't look as sad as he had before. Chris, the youngest of the three men kept his sandy blond hair trimmed. He has let his stubble grow and looks much older than he really is. Sarge is wearing black cargo pants and a compression shirt. He has been in his tactical gear apart from the vest since starting life at the cabin. He looks the most different. Not because he has lost weight or let his hair grow, but he is starting to be happy; a side of him no one has fully seen before.

"So, we have about a week's worth of food left from the last run." Chris tells them, scratching the hair on his face with his index and middle fingers.

"Mark, I know you have a soft spot in your heart for the people in the other cabin. But they need to do more for the group than what they have been." The old Sarge emerges.

Mark isn't too happy with the looks he's getting from the two other men in this three-man democracy, "So what, you want me to tell them to pack up and hit the road? 'Sorry you aren't helping, get your stuff and leave *your* cabin!' I don't think so."

Chris, being the cooler head, speaks up, "Ok look, all he's saying is tell them we need more help. I'm grateful for Manny going with me on supply runs, but he has three mouths to feed and only brings in enough for him."

This upsets Mark; he gets up off the edge of the bed and goes to the back window, "That's no one's fault, not much is out there anymore. I still can't wrap my head around all of this. People trying to eat you, that's bad enough... but the military opening fire on people... just normal people. I just don't—."

Chris stands, adjusts his blue jeans and t-shirt, he walks across the hard wood floor, his boots clunking the whole way, "You need to stop thinking about that day Mark. Saying this to you is like trying to milk an ant, as my daddy would say." Chris puts his hand on Mark's shoulder, "but I'm gonna anyway. You've lived through some bad stuff... we all have, but you have to let go."

Sarge brings them back to the task at hand, "Ok we need to send a team out to find more supplies and from the sounds of it we aren't going to find any around here." His cigar smoke fills the air. The sun peeking through the window catches the smoke twirling and swirling with every exhale. As Sarge rocks back and forth in the old rocking chair, he becomes shrouded in the smoke. In the sunlight, the smoke practically makes it a solid wall between Sarge and the tense men in the room with him.

Mark walks back to the bed and sits. It's an old handmade wooden frame. The wood carvings are that of a Native American's. Mark had to buy it when he saw it; the art was too beautiful to let it go to someone that would not appreciate it. The art on the wall matches it, but only in that it is western. Rachel didn't want art of people that had axes and bows and arrows. It would give her nightmares about being chased.

Mark looks around at the stone faces of the two votes against him and concedes the point, "Ok, so what? We give them some food and tell them to walk?"

"No, not at all. We bring Manny in on our little meetings and see what he thinks his family's role should be." Sarge smiles and puts his cigar in the glass ashtray overflowing with the butts of every cigar that didn't get destroyed months ago.

"Ok, fine by me." Mark rolls his eyes.

"That's grits with me." Chris says in a thicker accent than normal.

Both Sarge and Mark look at him, dumbfounded. Almost at the same time they say, "What the hell does that mean?"

Chris smiles and looks at both men, "Grits are good."

Everyone shakes their head, including Chris. His attempt to soften the mood fails.

Sarge picks up the cigar and tells Chris to go get Manny. As Chris leaves the back bedroom, Sarge catches a view of the living area through the now open door and notices a few more eyes than he'd like on him. He pushes the door closed and looks up at Mark who is now standing over a picture on the dresser.

"We going to talk about why you haven't left this cabin in almost a month?" Sarge's eyes cut Mark in half.

Mark picks up the picture, "You know as well as I do that, I'm no good out in the world anymore. After all that happened, I'm no help."

"That's bull and you know it!" Sarge stands.

"Don't raise your voice at me!" Mark takes a step closer, "I'm not one of your men in the trenches."

Sarge smiles and takes a step back, "Ok, ok, all I'm saying is I have seen you in action you're fine out there."

Mark goes on the defensive "I did what I had to, to keep my kids safe. They are safe now, so I need to keep them that wa—"

Sarge cuts him off, "If they starve to death, they ain't too safe."

Mark has no rebuttal. His eyes shoot toward the ground.

Sarge continues his verbal assault, "So you say you only did what you had to do. So, rolling over that guy Russ back on the highway in the beginning? That what you had to do?"

Mark fills with rage and sends evil eyes Sarge's way.

"Hey Chief, that sniper with the anger problems, that's my daughter. So, your pissed-off teenager looks do nothing to me." Sarge barks.

"So, what? You want me to go out into the world? What world?" Mark points out the window.

"There's that fire I saw when I met you on the street that night." Sarge takes a puff of his cigar and smiles while blowing the smoke Mark's way.

Mark opens his mouth to speak but a soft knock on the door stops him.

Chris pokes his head in, "Everything ok in here?"

Sarge turns to greet him, "Yea, five-by-five." Sarge walks back to the chair and sits.

Chris pushes the door the rest of the way open. He is followed in by Manny, a shorter guy who has black hair that's buzzed short on the sides.

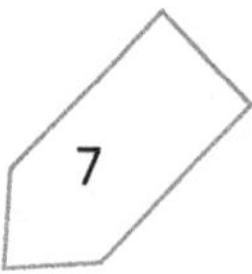

Sarge puffs on his cigar once more, "You're a plump little burrito, aren't you?" He blows the smoke in Manny's face.

"Was that a fat and a Mexican joke all in one?" Manny smiles.

Chris laughs, "I think a short joke too, he said, 'little'."

Manny, knowing he is in an on-the-spot interview, plays along fighting back anger, "So, did you invite me in here to make jokes or can I help you with something?"

Sarge, who isn't comfortable with Manny's bluntness continues puffing on his cigar and smiles a sideways grin, "That's what I want to know. Can you help with something?" Sarge points at Manny with the cigar slowly burning between his index and middle fingers. He is still sitting in the rocking chair next to the door.

Manny looks around the room suspicious of this being a setup. He looks long at Mark, trying to read him, "I can try and help anyway I can."

Sarge stops rocking to pull out his handgun and places it on the waist-high oak table, the barrel pointing at Manny. He starts to rock again, his face disappearing behind the smoke every time he rocks back.

Mark has had enough of the games, "Ok, here's the deal, we want you to pull a little more—" Sarge cuts Mark off. "Everyone plays; no one sits. That is the way this works. *WE* need you to do a little more for us."

Manny looks around the room once more, "More like what?"

Sarge looks at Manny, "You already go on runs with the ex, over there." Sarge cuts a look at Chris who has accepted his months old nickname, being ex-Army it isn't an insult, "So that will still happen, but as we don't know you or what you know, we want you to be a part of these meetings we have." Now Sarge has a diabolical smirk on his face, "Find ways you can help. Everyone has a skill set; you just have to find yours. Take Mark, he had a cabin and has a talent for drawing, so if we needed a map or something like that he could come in handy. The ex, he... well he's useful. So, you just need to find what you're good at besides eating." Sarge puts the cigar out in the ash tray.

Chris speaks up, "Right now we are low on supplies and need to go on a run, but a bit bigger than normal."

Manny rubs his head, "Man, you've been out there. Most of the towns are burnt and any place that isn't has been picked clean."

"Manny, you're thinking on a small scale. That's what I bring. We need to get gear that will keep us alive here and make it unnecessary to go out as often." Sarge tells him.

"So, what did you have in mind?" Mark asks.

Sarge stands and looks out the window, "We haven't had much Zeek activity up here, so maybe they did move east and west, or the firebombing did its job. Either way we can fortify this place, or we can move. I say we got water, we have a safe place to sleep, and power off the grid. We need walls or a fence, we also need early warning systems. Stuff like that." Sarge turns back to the room and looks at Chris, "You know what I'm talking about?"

Chris nods his head, "Yeah, I get the idea. So, Manny and I go and get this stuff, and get whatever we see, and feel can help."

"Yep, that's the idea. Is that good with you, Manny?" Sarge asks.

Manny seeing the opportunity to insert himself into the group nods his head "Yeah, that's fine with me."

Sarge pulls keys out of his cargo pocket, "Take my truck. You'll have more room to put stuff in the bed if we pull the camper shell off." He tosses the keys to Mark.

"Why are you giving these to me?" Mark hands the keys to Chris.

"You're going too! You know what would work with the power grid of this house to expand it to some of the other cabins so we all have power and may know of places Manny doesn't." Sarge looks Mark in the eyes.

Mark, unable to argue that point, rolls his eyes and walks out of the room. Manny follows and both men go to their families.

Sarge stops Chris to make one last request. "We need Mark back. He's too useful to go scared turtle on us now. Don't take it easy on him out there."

Chris hesitates to respond, "Ok. You think he'll be happy to talk to me? With me and Evelyn being whatever we are now."

"Better his daughter than mine." Sarge smiles and pushes Chris out the door, laughing.

Mark's son, Ryan and Manny's daughter, Grace, are out by the lake. Mark is looking at her, noticing her long dark hair blowing in the cool late fall breeze. Her plump cheeks, rosy from the chill in the air, make her look younger than Ryan when she is a year older than him. Mark watches them as they toss rocks into the lake seeing who can get the farthest throw. The rocks hit the water and they laugh.

Mark thinks to himself: *Must be nice to find the little things still fun. I can't stop seeing those jets coming, the heat from the fires, and the feeling of Evelyn's hands slipping out of mine. What is Sarge trying to do? I will go and come back, and he will have moved all my stuff out and take the cabin. No, Mark, don't think like that; you can trust him. He saved your life; he wouldn't do that.*

Chris hollers, "Hey Mark, let's hit it!"

Mark walks up to the black truck that is in almost every way the opposite of his. This Loud, and over the top, Sarge's being the biggest of the two. Evelyn walks up behind him and hugs him. He turns to her and before he can look into her eyes that remind him of her mother, she shoots around the truck and jumps into Chris's arms. Mark looks at them and smiles but hides it quickly. Mark opens the door and gets in. Chris does the same. Manny is already in the back seat because he took off the camper shell ahead of time.

Sarge almost sarcastically calls out, "I'll keep them safe!"

"Ok boss, I got your back out here." Chris smiles at Mark happy to have him at his side again.

"I'm not your boss, not anymore. Just drive and let's get this done." Mark looks down at the rifle in his lap, eyes sad and heart beating hard and fast. This is the first time he's held this one since the attack on the hospital. The last time he fired a gun was on the road when Dave, someone he thought of as his brother, and who had been his best friend, attacked the group.

Chris is driving down the access road that leads them back to the main road from the cabins, the sunlight flickering through the holes where leaves had once soaked up that very same sunlight. Chris is overjoyed as evident by the huge smile on his face. Being back behind the wheel of a pickup truck and even more so, because of the power and ability to go fast over the bumps.

Chris, with his southern accent, "Man, it's been years since I could have fun on a dirt road like this."

They get to the brush that blocks the opening to the main road. Mark gets out, as does Manny, who keeps an eye out while Mark moves the branches. Chris drives onto the main road and Mark, putting the branches back, looks at Manny to ease his own mind.

Back in the truck , Mark sees that the firebombing did less damage to this area. *Maybe it's because they didn't think people lived this far out.*

They reach the outskirts of the town after a short drive; the streets are black and most of the cars are melted heaps of metal. Some areas have trees others have blackened trunks and ash covering the ground. Chris is driving fast, Manny has fallen asleep in the back seat, a bit of drool on his cheek, but Mark has his eyes glued to the road ahead looking for anything to ensure this trip will be over sooner rather than later.

The trees become rubble and the rubble becomes burnt houses. They have reached the heart of the closest town to the cabin.

"This is the first place we looked through for anything useful." Chris says slowing down to take a closer look, "Not much here but ash now."

"I wonder how many people were still here when it happened." Manny pops up from the back seat.

Chris looks out the window at what looks as if it could have been a church, "Let's look here really quick and see if there's any canned food or anything else like that inside. I don't think we checked this one out."

Mark reluctantly gets out, and by the look on Manny's face he too thinks it's not worth the time.

"In and out, we need to go to where they may have been expanding the town." Mark says, closing the door quietly.

"Why there, Mark?" Manny asks, stepping over large beams that must have rolled out as the fire ripped through it.

"We need building supplies and that's where they'd be. Steel maybe. That would be the best thing to find." Mark tells him.

Chris walks ahead to check and see if inside is safe or not. Mark bends down and uses the barrel of the rifle to push the rubble and debris around. The sun reflects off something that shines through the ashes in the burnt building. Mark bends down to pick it up.

"What's that?" Manny asks.

"Don't know, looks like a coin of some kind." Mark rubs the ash off with his thumb and tries to read the words, "It is a coin. It has writing on it like an award maybe."

"Hey guys, in here!" Chris's voice bellows out of the fractured building. The quiet is unsettling.

Mark and Manny run inside. Chris is standing in front of a safe with a big spinning handle, "So that's what this is, it's a bank."

Chris and Mark start to look around. Seat frames with tattered fabric on the edges and desks folded in from the heat of the fire that had ripped this place apart. A loud series of clicks comes from the back of what was the tellers' desk.

APRIL

Mark and Chris turn to see Manny playing with the safe, "Sorry guys, I always wanted to do that." Manny takes a step back.

Chris and Mark go back to looking, "You're proving your helpful right?" Chris jokes.

Manny doesn't find it funny but laughs cynically. He returns to searching, "What are we doing? We aren't going to find anything in here. Ash and burnt money won't help us."

Snarls echo from behind them. All three men swing toward the safe, its door is inching open. Chris waves at the other two to fan out. The door is heavy and solid, hard to move.

"Whatever it is isn't too strong, maybe it's only one." Manny smiles optimistically.

The door opens far enough that hands can fit through the crack. First one hand then two. Then more than can be counted. Chris yells, "Outside, now! Move! Move! Move!"

They rush outside and stop at the truck, "What are we doing? Let's get out of here." Manny starts to open the door of the truck.

"No, we set them free. We have to stop them from hurting anyone." Mark slams the door shut.

"Who? It's just us out here." Manny gripes back.

"Mark's right, what if someone's holed up in the woods or something and they get loose on them?" Chris agrees.

The first of the Zeeks start to stumble out of the wreckage. They look like bankers and maybe people that came in that day, when they or someone locked them in there. POP! The decrepit body hit the ground. POP! The next one's head explodes, leaving coagulated blood all over the next few in line.

"There must have been ten of those things in there." Manny calls out.

POP! POP! POP! Chris fires more shots into the group of bobbing heads. Mark grits his teeth and steps up beside Chris. He starts to take aim, face tight and full of anger and regret. That first shot feels alien to him, even still it hit its target. The next trigger pull comes easier. Seeing the Zeek's head explode however, never gets any less disturbing for Mark. The familiarity of gunfire puts Mark back in a groove and this messed up world feels right again.

The ten or so Zeeks that had spilled out now cover the ground, as thick as the ash. Manny hadn't even fired a shot. Chris walks over to the pile and checks to make sure they are all dead for good.

"We should go look in the safe. They could have had food in there." Mark starts to walk back to the door.

"No way. What could be in there? I'm not eating anything we find in there." Manny folds his arms.

"Fine, watch the car. Mark and I will check it out." Chris says while checking the magazine in his gun.

Mark and Chris start up the scorched stone stairs. They walk, stepping over the dead, some of whom look as if they had been eating each other. They have bites taken out of limbs, necks, and faces. The safe door is wide open and empty of anything moving. It's dark inside the safe. Chris turns on the flashlight attached to his gun. The beam lights up the small, shiny room. Safety deposit boxes line the sides of the room but on the rearmost wall are shelves that look like they had been used as beds or something. After a longer look, there is a child's body on the ground in the very back corner. She is curled up in a tight ball behind the shelves.

"Crap! That's a little kid..." Chris holds his light on her, "she is maybe what? Five?"

Mark walks to the body, he kneels, "She doesn't look like she has any bites..." Sadness fills his voice, "I think she may have just starved to death." Mark looks at this small girl. Her skin is tight and stretched over her bones of which you can see all. Mark finds this hard to take in. After his long look, he walks to a shelf and grabs a blanket.

He wraps the girl's coiled body within it. On her right wrist is a bracelet with plastic beads that spell out April. Mark carries her outside and sets her on a spot that isn't completely burned. He then starts to place planks around her, and Chris joins him. They aren't covering her but encasing her in a crypt. Once this is done, they take a moment then set back out on their search.

Almost half the day is gone, but they haven't gotten anything worthwhile. Manny tells them about the new hotel that was started but never opened, "It's about another ten minutes from here on the far side of town. It was set to open this month, but that's not going to happen now."

"Why didn't you tell me that before? We could have started there!" Chris is angrier with the wasted time more than anything.

"Sorry, I just remembered it." Manny sinks in his seat.

"Well, let's go check it out." Mark speaks for the first time since leaving little April.

Chris drives the ten minutes unimpeded. They arrive at a big building that is three quarters of the way finished, "This place is big Manny!" Chris looks up at this four-story building, "No way we can get that place looked through today with just the three of us."

"Agreed, we would need Sarge and Angel to get that done."
Mark says.

"I say we drive home, tell them, and come back loaded with
both trucks, and get everything we can." Chris scans the car for
differing ideas, he receives none.

"Ok, sounds good to me. Let's hit it and get back to the cabin."
Mark tries not to seem so overjoyed. The vision of the cabin so
vivid in his head he could almost touch it, feel its warmth even.

Chris turns the truck around and points it at the road home,
"Manny, you have any other ideas that we can check out now?"

"Not at the moment, but I'll think about it." Manny replies.

 # Fires Within

The truck pulls down the narrow dirt road to the cabin. Chris stops the truck halfway. He rolls down the window and jokingly waves a napkin as if it were a white flag. Chris steps out of the truck, "Angel of Death! We have news. Grab a ride back?"

Chris stands, looking up at the treetops. A pinecone hits him in the back of the head. Angel is a third of the way up in a tree stand posted just to the side of the road in a mid-weight grey coat. Working on sharpening sticks, "I like the white flag, it was a nice touch. So, about that ride?" She starts down the tree. Her blond hair is shorter than it was in the summer.

"We found a place that will take all of us to cover." Chris opens the back door for Angel, "when we fill Sarge in you'll hear it." She leans down under his muscular arm, Chris smiles and closes the door.

Back at the cabin, no one is outside. This seems odd to Mark. As the car doors close, Evelyn flies out of the cabin, "Come quick! Come!" She waves the group on.

Angel doesn't start to run like the rest, she takes her time. Once inside, the sound of a voice on a TV is unmistakable. Mark, Chris, Manny, and Angel all stand behind the dark brown couch looking at the TV.

"What? How did you...?" Mark can't find his words.

"Dad, I was playing the old video games and when I stopped, it was on channel three. This voice came on." Ryan points to the TV.

The TV is on the Emergency Alert System screen, a computerized female voice reciting: This Is not a test. If you are receiving this message you are inside the outbreak zone. Please stay in your homes if possible. Help is coming. Message will repeat on the hour.

"Ha-Ha-Ha. Help is coming. Help is coming from where? From whom? The same people that firebombed us and that city?" Sarge puffs on his cigar.

"Must you do that?" Elsa waves her hand, dispersing the smoke.

"He has a point." Mark sits in another beat up chair in the room.

"What point? They say help is coming. Maybe the firebombing did the trick. Maybe they got them all." Elsa says, pushing her long dark brown hair behind her ear, hope in her eyes.

"What do you guys think? You were just out there, did they get 'em all or is it still hell on earth?" Sarge scans the room with piercing eyes, "What, no answer? Nobody? Joey you feel all safe and protected?"

Joey walks into the tense room. He shrugs his shoulders and looks to Mark. He seems tired of Sarge's jokes.

Chris steps up, "From what I saw, it could be better out there, but we've only been a few miles out. Big cities could still be overrun."

"Elsa, it doesn't seem as if it's any different to me." Manny hugs his wife to soften the blow of this news. The room gets cold and silent.

"When you pulled up, you said you had news." Angel changes the subject.

"Oh yeah, we found a hotel. Still being built. The kind of place we could find what we need to make defenses." Marks's eyes cut a hole into Sarge.

"Sounds good. We'll check it out tomorrow." Sarge stands and walks toward Angel. "Joey will help this time, get him helping out."

Angel follows Sarge to the window overlooking the lake, "You want me to pack it in for the day? Seems like it will be all hands-on deck tomorrow." Angel asks looking up at Sarge. Her look is soft for once.

"Your call. If you want to come in, that's fine by me. The less you're out there alone the better. If those things catch a whiff of our scent this close to camp, who knows." Sarge, speaking metaphorically, looks out the window long and hard.

"What is it, Dad?" Angel now growing concerned.

"Every time I think we are alone and safe, someone makes contact. Russ, the call on Evelyn's voicemail. I want to think the U.S. government wouldn't just leave us to die, but my years of duty tell me differently. I've seen them send a chopper for a guy with no legs and one arm, hell, half his damn head split open, then leave a six-man unit to fend for themselves." Sarge turns to look at his little girl, the lady sniper. "Angel you are all I have in this world. The last thing I want is to lose you, or worse, leave you alone."

"Dad, you're scaring me. What is going on?" Angel puts her hand on the large, somber man.

"Baby girl, I know we have seen and done worse, but I just can't help but think things are about to get spun around on us."

"Hey, Marine! You get your head back in it. I don't want to hear you talk like that again. We are not alone here, we have friends, heck I'd even say family. You think Meg wants to hear you talk like that?" Angel pokes fun at the not-so-secret relationship.

Sarge smiles and hugs Angel big and tight, picking her up, "10-4, copy that. This old man is just going soft. I think I must need to shoot something."

Sarge puts Angel down and walks to Mark, kicking Chris's foot along the way, "Come fill me in on what happened out there."

Manny looks at the men, "Should I come in there, too?"

Sarge is the last one through the door. Just before he kicks it shut, he says, "Not so much." SLAM! The old, solid wood door shakes the picture frames on the wall.

On the other side of the door, Mark asks, "Was that necessary?"

Sarge smiles, "Yes it was. I need him to think we still don't trust him."

Mark takes a seat on the bed, as he does the springs creak and moan. Chris stands at the window looking out at a string with tin cans on it. The three of them have drifted apart after the months of being stuck around one another. Chris turns and looks at Sarge, almost saddened.

"Why does he need to think that? Don't we trust him?" Chris takes a seat in the old wooden rocking chair just in front of the window.

"Well, how'd he do out there?" Sarge gets to the point.

 Mark cuts a look at Chris then back at Sarge, "He didn't do great, but it was his idea about the hotel."

 "That's something, I guess. You know his wife is dead weight, right?" Sarge lights his cigar the ting and snap of the opening and closing of his lighter put off an intimidating vibe. "The sooner we can get Joey back out there the better."

 "Why? She helps around here, right? Her, Meg, and Ev have kept things neat and livable." Mark gets up and walks through the cigar smoke. "Joey isn't ready." Mark looks at the ground, "He still needs time. You treating him like he's a kid faking sick isn't helping."

 Chris is growing tired of Sarge's games and Mark's lack of motivation, "You two have lost it; I'm sick of whatever this is. Here's the plan for tomorrow. Sarge, Manny, and Joey take one half of the hotel. Mark, Ev, and I will take the other. Angel will set up somewhere close to keep anything from sneaking up on us. Can you handle that or is this going to be a fight, too?" Chris's voice hits a harsh tone no one has heard before.

 "I like it Ex, that fire, that bark, it's what you need to keep his little girl in line. Something she's never seen before I'd guess." Sarge smirks at Mark hoping for a reaction.

 Mark doesn't take the bait, "Yeah Chris, it is something you need. Be your own man don't follow either one of us."

 "God damnit you two, you are both... you both offer something to this group, but when it's like this you hurt us all!" Chris walks out of the room. Leaving the door open. The rest of this splintered group looks on and can feel the tension spill out of the room like a tidal wave.

Mark doesn't move from his spot. Sarge starts to walk out before he takes two steps on the creaky floor, Chris stops him by putting his hand on Sarge's chest, "If you ever talk about Evelyn like that again, Mark won't be your problem." Chris's eyes don't leave Sarge's dark brown eyes as they look back at him, his point is made and Sarge steps back with his hands up. Everyone in the room is silent. Sarge goes to one of the bedrooms and Meg follows. Evelyn is unsure whether to go to her father or Chris. This decision is made easy as Angel goes into the room with Mark. Evelyn follows Chris out the front door. She stops and looks at Ryan playing with Grace. He shoots her a quick, "it's ok", smile. She wraps her arms around Chris's waist as they walk out. These three Titans needing to retreat to neutral corners before their small world suffers more devastation.

"Mark, what's going on with him?" Angel asks, practically falling on the bed.

"I don't know Angel. He hasn't been the same in weeks. He and I always butted heads but now it's on a different level." Mark puts his hand on Angel's back as she looks at the nicks in the old dark oak floor. Her blond hair falling beside her face.

"I have never seen him like this. It scares me to death. He was always the guy stuck on go..." She pauses and chokes back tears. "Even when my brother left, he was off to train new recruits the next day. 'Keep safe and watch your six, girl,' is what he said to me."

"I think he could just be waiting for the other shoe to drop. He'll come around." Mark consoles the crumbling, humbled girl.

Angel sniffles and wipes her eyes. The redness makes her gray eyes sharp, almost piercing, "You don't think it's all this Meg stuff, do you?" She asks looking Mark right in the eyes.

"No. I think that is doing more good than bad, maybe he doesn't want to fall for her." Mark hugs Angel and stands her up.

"Thanks Mark, I feel like I'm not the only one seeing him be different. Oh, what was that thing with him and Chris about?" She asks, still in the hug.

"Oh, he said some stuff trying to get a rise out of me, it didn't work." Their eyes meet as they pull away, locking in on each other in a new way. Her gray eyes still sharp, breaking through his hardened brown eyes. He smiles at her and shows her out of the room and closes the door. Mark is beat and hasn't had time to decompress from the encounter earlier. He takes slow, heavy steps to the bed, he kicks off his ashy, blood covered boots, and pulls off his shirt. All the manual labor of these last few months has gotten him into better shape. His pants come off next, frayed jeans that he found in a closet most likely left on a happy trip, memories of which now escape him. He drops on the bed.

November 24, 2011

The smell of Thanksgiving cooking fills the house, Mark opens his eyes and he is back in his bed in his house. A smile appears on his face as his eyes go to the long, dark wooden dresser; pictures of his family and his wife greet his eyes.

Wearing a white tee shirt and light blue pajama pants, swinging his legs out of bed and down into his faux fur lined slippers. Mark starts to walk the hard wood floors. They are almost glowing in the morning light. He walks past Evelyn's room first; she is still sound asleep. Before he gets to the bathroom, he stops by Ryan's room. The door is cracked and Mark peeks in to see Ryan building a plastic block fortress.

Mark grabs his toothbrush and looks in the mirror as he starts to brush, seeing the happy in his eyes. He looks down to spit and when he brings his head up, behind him stands Rachel. Her dark blue camisole and almost see through white linen pants catch his eye. She looks young and healthy because this is months before the cancer took hold again. She smiles at Mark, her flowing blond hair framing her face making her look like an angel as the bright bathroom light hits it. She walks up behind him, wraps her arms around Mark's waist and hugs him. He can feel her warmth pressing against him.

As he turns to her, he leans down for a kiss and their lips meet. Her lips are soft and smooth like silk. Long passionate kisses turn to short smiling ones.

Mark pulls away just a little his eyes still closed, "What's so funny?" He says softly.

Rachel kisses him one more time and slides her hand from behind his back' "This." She wipes her hand covered in raw turkey juice over his face.

Mark angry, but still every bit in love, grabs Rachel and pulls her up and in, rubbing his turkey juice covered face all over hers. Her laugh is playful and sweet. When Mark stops, their eyes lock and both are filled with a fire that consumes them. Hard kisses lead to Mark picking Rachel up, wrapping his hands around her full thighs and setting her on the bathroom counter. His kisses start on her lips then drift down to her neck. Rachel leans her head back, closing her eyes bracing herself with her hands on the edge of the counter.

Mark's kisses have started to land on Rachel's chest, her thin-strapped top is starting to get in Mark's way. He pushes one strap to the side, replacing it with kisses. He moves to the other strap, and by this time most of Rachel's top is around her midsection. Mark places a few more kisses in important places before looking into Rachel's brilliant green eyes. Rachel overcome with emotion, pulls Mark in by the strings on his pajama pants.

She starts to undo the knot; Mark starts kissing her neck. The smell of her hair is intoxicating to Mark. Rachel slides her hands in the back of his pants, squeezing his butt, then slips the pants off. Mark looks in the mirror and sees his face, but it's covered in rotting flesh and his eyes have blood streaming down them.

He steps back, startled, and everything is back to normal, but he can hear Evelyn's voice and knocks at the door. Rachel hands Mark his pants, smacks his butt, and leans into his ear, "We will finish this later." She bites his ear as she pulls away with a smile.

"Dad! Wake up, Dad!" Evelyn's voice truly calls out.

Mark Opens his eyes to see Evelyn and Angel standing in his room of the cabin.

Angel smiles and covers her mouth, "Is that... Good dream?"

Mark looks down and notices he's on display from under the sheets; embarrassed, he slides his hands down to cover himself.

Evelyn, too embarrassed, covers her eyes, "Eww Dad!" She walks to the door.

Angel, not shaken one bit, "We're getting ready to go look around that hotel, so put that away and meet us by the trucks."

 # Hotel Party

Mark has made his way to the living room and Joey stops him, handing him a note.

Sorry it's been so long. I've never wanted to be dependent on other people. After almost getting Chris eaten, I just kind of didn't want to be around anyone.

Mark looks at Joey, slightly saddened that he never considered how everyone waiting on him could hurt. Also feeling bad he hasn't become better at sign language, so he doesn't need to write notes.

It's ok, you have your reasons. I'm just glad you're doing good.

Joey puts some snacks in his pocket and adjusts his baggy jeans.

You think I'm useful, don't you?

Of course, I do, Joey. More than me right now.

Well, I just don't want to be in the way or useless... You know?

Trust me, you're fine. I bet Sarge will be happy to go do this thing with you and not me.

He did ask for me to help him out. Are you two butting heads again?

Joey turns to Mark who is still standing. Mark starts to walk to the window, seeing the group loading up and ready to spring into action.

You know, sometimes I think I could have made it here without his help. Then I remember that we all had the same goal, so what does it matter?

Joey walks to Mark and reads the last thing Mark wrote. With soft eyes and a smile Joey writes.

None of us would be here if it wasn't for you, Sarge included. You brought us all together. I will always remember the guy that could have killed me and didn't. Instead he put me in his car and took me to a place that was safe. Of course, I was almost eaten, got shot, bout got cut open and experimented on, but, you know, it ended up good. :)

Mark reads and smiles, "You are such an ass, you know that? But thanks, you just helped me a lot."

Joey reads Mark's lips then smiles at Mark; the two walk out to the trucks, joining the others. The cold air smells of lake and winter.

Sarge has already laid out a plan, "Nice of you to join us sleeping beauty. Now that Mark is here, let's go over this again. Ex, Evelyn and Mark, you guys look for food and water. Also get bedding. You know, sheets and any blankets, its already feeling like winter at night." Sarge speaking down to Mark in a condescending voice, "Joey and I will grab building supplies and anything we can make into a defense system. A half-day drive there and a half day's drive back doesn't leave much time to work, so no wasting time."

Mark looks at Chris and Evelyn, both nod their heads in agreement, but oddly still found himself wanting Joey with him, "So if you guys need help or we need it, what's the plan for that?" Mark asks.

"Well, Angel will keep watch; we shouldn't run into too much out there, I'd think, with that firebombing and overall lack of food." Sarge says with too much confidence on his face.

"Where do you want me?" Angel asks, pulling her hair back.

"Down low, not too high, so if we need your support it's there." Sarge replies as he slaps a magazine in his rifle.

Manny looks around and sees everyone has a weapon but him, "Do I get a gun, or do you still not trust me?"

Sarge looks at Manny as he opens the door to his truck, "You, with a weapon behind me? Sorry, I'll pass." Sarge hands Joey his pistol, smiling.

"Be careful, baby." Elsa kisses Manny and Grace hugs them both, her arms barley reaching around the two of them together.

Ryan hugs Evelyn and Chris. He walks up to Mark, "Dad, when you get back, can we go for a walk?"

"Sure, Ryan, as long as you're good for Meg and Elsa." Mark kneels to Ryan's height, looking him in his almost mirror-like eyes.

"Dad, I'm going to read about animal tracks and stuff while you're gone and point stuff out like we did... before... does that sound fun?" Ryan's excitement fills the air.

"Sounds great, son." HONK! HONK! Sarge has grown even more impatient, "I've got to go now. Keep the ladies safe, ok?"

Mark gets into his truck. Sarge leads the way in his loud, over-the-top truck. Joey, Angel, and Manny ride along with him. Mark prepares himself for the task at hand. So much so, that as Sarge slows, Mark almost rear ends him.

"Dad, are you ok?" Evelyn asks from the back seat.

Mark hesitates briefly, "I'm ok. I just hope this goes as easy as we hope it will."

"We're golden, boss." Chris adds, with his charming Texas accent.

"Chris, I'm not your boss anymore. You don't work for me. That life is dead now." Mark looks over at Chris who is looking at Evelyn in the sideview mirror, "You are your own person and, from the look of it, going steady with my daughter." Mark smiles awaiting the bashful Evelyn's response.

"Oh my God, dad! No one even says that anymore. I'm glad you can joke about it, just hope you're this ok with it when the baby gets here..." Evelyn looks at the floor of the truck.

"WHAT? You're..." Mark is at a loss for words.

Evelyn can't hold her laughter back anymore, "Not so funny now, is it Dad?"

"Ev can you not provoke him while he's driving, and my life is in his hands?" Chris jokes keeping the light mood going.

Mark, happy that he has gotten a better relationship with Evelyn, can't help but smile. "Ev, I can't even tell you how much you remind me of her. It seems lately it's been all I can do not to call you Rachel sometimes." Mark looks to see if he just put a damper on the mood in the truck.

Before anyone has time to feel sad, they quickly pull up on the hotel's mostly finished parking lot. A large four-story hotel, it looks like a dark stained log cabin with a green shingled roof. It seems to be mostly finished but still has construction equipment and a chain link fence around it. Overall, after looking around, this area seems unaffected by the fires. No ash no burnt anything; in fact, it looks like life stood still here.

Sarge waves Mark on to back in first and after Mark gets his truck backed in, Sarge follows. Again, they form a V so if something swarms them from the outside, they may be able to fight a way out. As the group unloads, Sarge sees a few of the construction pick-up trucks with dust on them as if they haven't moved for a while. Joey starts that way, Sarge stops him.

"Hey Manny, I got a job for you." Sarge smiles.

"And what's that? Let me guess, bait?" Manny gripes at the still smiling Sarge.

"No, Buddy. You see the three trucks over there?" Sarge points as he puts his hand on Manny's back. "We need to see if they have gas, and if they do, we need it." Sarge pulls out a rubber hose from a duffle bag.

Manny looks at the hose, "How do I do that?"

"Syphon it out. I bet you're really good at sucking, too." Sarge hands Manny the hose, pushing it hard to his chest with a thud.

"So, you want me to suck the gas out of them? Then what? What do I put it in?" Manny holds his real comments back.

"Just look around for anything you can use, this is a construction site after all." Sarge walks toward the front doors bringing Joey with him.

Mark and his group are a few steps behind. Looking up at this tall wooden structure, Mark can't help but think it will be overrun inside. *Food, water, bedding, food, water, bedding. All I need to do, is get that and get out. Keep Ev and me safe. Chris and I will be ok in here, but her? I don't like this. I don't want this for her. Look at her, she's basically a doughy-eyed teenager. I guess Chris will take better care of her given the way they feel about each other. Rachel, watch over us in here....*

Chris pops a piece of gum in his mouth and hands Mark a piece, "Eat it, it will keep you from clenching your jaw and give you something to do while we try and move about this happy-wrapped nightmare we are about to walk into."

"My jaw?" Mark starts to chew.

"Yeah, when you start to get nervous or worried your jaw clenches. This will keep you calm. Trust me, my partner did the same thing, and this helped him tons." Chris says as he puts a knife in his boot.

"Ok gang!" Sarge says getting everyone's attention with a stern voice. "Let's do this. Tight, silent, and fast gets us home. Only use your bullets if you have to, everyone has a blade, use them." Sarge gets the group moving to the doors with a wave of his hand.

Mark and his team start into the hotel, it's dark inside as the sun is on the back side of the building. The interior isn't as finished as it was on the exterior, some of the walls aren't painted and some flooring is missing. The further they get, the more the light fades. Mark turns on his flashlight and starts down a hallway, doors run the length. Chris and Evelyn are side-by-side behind him. Chris turns and walks backward every few steps. The first door they come to is on the left of the hallway, no room number or indication of what could be inside, Mark stops with the flashlight on it.

Mark waves his hand instructing them to go in, "I'll open it; Chris you go in first and Ev you stay out here and make sure nothing comes up behind us." Mark whispers in the white-blue flashlight glow.

"Dad, I can help. I didn't come out here to just stand around." Evelyn insists.

"I know kid, but we need someone to watch the hall and Chris can kill things better than anyone I know." Mark looks up at Chris.

"I think that was a compliment, Ev, I agree with him; you are more important than what may or may not be behind this door. We will go in and you can keep us safe if we mess up." Chris hugs her and kisses her forehead.

"Ok, side note: Chris, I get the forehead. If you kiss her there, what do I do after?" Mark smiles.

Evelyn blushing, "Dad, that was just weird."

"Yeah, now you see how I feel. Moving on, let's do this." Mark gets set at the door taking a deep breath of musty air with a hint of something more.

As the door swings open, Chris steps in, immediately gagging at the smell, and begins to cover his face. Mark is next in and becomes overwhelmed with the number of flies swarming. As the swarm thins, the body of a woman is seen hanging from the unfinished ceiling feet barely off the ground. Chris looks at Mark to verify this is real. Mark, trying to keep his eyes off the body, sees a duffle bag on the floor in the corner of the room and goes to it.

After getting the bag, Mark starts out of the room. He takes one last look at the body as if to offer his respect. He puts the bag on the nicely finished real wood floor and opens the zipper. Before he can open it all the way odd noises echo from the room. Mark turns to find the source of the sounds, now the three are looking at the lifeless body reawakening. Thrashing about her eyes almost bulging out of her head about to burst, this catches Mark, Evelyn and Chris off guard.

"What do we do dad?" Evelyn is visibly shaken.

Mark stands to take care of the problem, the sound of the rope getting tighter around her neck and the stifled grunts give Mark pause. He takes one more step toward the pendulum like body and the problem takes care of itself. The weight of her decomposing body coupled with the thrashing about causes her body to fall from her head like over ripe fruit from a tree.

The smell let loose is infinitely worse than when they walked into the room. Evelyn waving her hand franticly in front of her face and panicked asks, "Dad, can we get out of here now?"

Chris reaches for her hand, "I second that request. Let's keep moving."

Mark seeing his role as the protector and knight in shining armor fading, is silent. The small group leaves, Mark closing the door to the room returning to the hallway. Mark has the duffle bag on his back and brings up the rear as Chris leads. Mark can see that his little girl is trying with everything she has to keep moving. Thinking to himself, *maybe it was a bad idea to let her come? I know she's not six anymore... hell she's not even sixteen anymore. Keeping her away from this world would only hurt her; she needs to be out here; she needs to see what it's like to be in danger, so she isn't shocked by it if she ends up alone. She's my little girl and will always be my little girl. I just hope she isn't trying to impress Chris... or even worse me. She is so much like Rachel, strong but unknowingly so. GOD, I miss you Rachel.*

"Mark, did you see that?" Chris calls back snapping Mark back to reality.

"No, what was it?" Mark scans the Dark interior hallway.

Chris takes two more small steps and stops dead in his tracks. With a whisper, "We are not alone." He reaches back placing his hand gently on Evelyn's waist. The hallway opens into a common area the majority of the natural light is coming from it. As they stand on the right side and peer into the light looking for whatever is lurking about. A rustling coming from the end of hall grabs the attention of all three.

"Sounds like its coming from the second to last door on the right. Let's move." Chris waves Mark up and to the left.

Taking the risk Mark slowly walks down the left side of the hall attempting to see into the room. As he gains a working vantage point, he now calls Evelyn and Chris up. Chris pulls his shotgun to his shoulder as he slides up to the door frame. Mark shakes his head saying he can't see anything. Mark takes one more step to his left and can now see all the way into the room with only the far-right corner being hidden from his sight.

Evelyn raises her pistol clicking the safety off. The rustling becomes much more panicked. Evelyn looks at the two frozen men, "I think who or whatever it is, is afraid like you two." Evelyn pushes past Chris and into the room gun at the ready.

Her jocular voice floats out of the room, "You two big, bad, zombie killing men need to get in here."

They follow her instruction only to find Evelyn laughing and pointing at a storage shelf that has tube rack-type shelves and is almost to the ceiling. On it is a raccoon trying to find its way down but too afraid to take the next leap.

"And you two were all worked up over this cute little guy?" Evelyn giggles.

"Cute? I don't think so. Those things have rabies." Chris scoffs.

"I'm with him, that thing is filthy." Mark ruffles his brow and curls his lip.

Now, looking around the room, it is a linen closet. Sheets and pillowcases on one side, and comforters and towels on the other. "Jackpot! Ok Evelyn, you stay here and get as much of this into those laundry bags as you can. You'll have your new friend to keep you safe." Mark smiles at her, "Chris and I will go look for the kitchen. If you need us, use your radio."

"Ok dad. You guys sure you don't need me to lead the way?" She smirks back.

"Yeah, yeah, you just be safe. Ok Mark, let's do this." Chris starts to walk to the door, stopping to kiss Evelyn on the cheek. Mark smiles and Chris taps Evelyn on the forehead smiling at Mark. Not going to pass up the moment to show affection to his little girl in today's world, he kisses Evelyn. They set off down the hall toward the common area. As they walk swiftly and quietly, an odd feeling runs down Mark's spine. He takes one more step and grabs Chris on the shoulder.

"Stop. I have a bad feeling about this." Mark whispers.

Not one to take unnecessary risks, Chris picks up a disregarded bottle off the floor and tosses it out into the open area ahead. Before it hits the ground. BANG! A shot rings out that sends the bottle flying in a different direction. Both Mark and Chris get flat against the wall.

Evelyn leans out into the hall to investigate the gunshot. She gets a commanding wave to get back into the storage closet. Nonetheless she stands at the ready to protect her men if need be.

"Mark, this guy is a good shot and I think that shot came from up high, stairs maybe; all I know is he has us pinned down. I'm going to move to the other side of the hall and see if I can find the shooter." As Chris finishes his plan, he hops across the hall and inches his way to a vantage point just before the wall ends. His eyes grow large, he dives back toward the cover of the hall. Not a moment too soon because as he hits the ground, a second shot strikes the wall where his head would have been.

Mark is shaken, but his fast thinking kicks in. "Ok!" He yells. "You got us, but I'm sure the three of us are on the same side here, right?" Mark calls out to this marksman.

An older man's voice replies, "Don't you mean the four of us? I heard a gal's voice, too." A hint of sarcasm is detected.

Mark prepares to speak; Chris moves his hand in a circular motion saying to keep it going. "Ok, you're right, we have three people; we are just looking for some food and supplies just like you." "Well, that was strike one. We only play to one strike around these parts, so you best quit your lies." The backwoods accent starts to emerge from the man.

"Ok, whatever you say, sir. I was never much for baseball. How's about we all come to where we can see each other?"

Mark looks at Chris who has been on the radio to the rest of the group.

"Ya'll toss your weapons out here on the floor, slowly. Then come out with your hands laced and on your head." The man orders.

The trio does just that. They slowly walk out into the open, setting eyes on this mystery man. He is of average height and build; he has large eyes, made bigger by the situation no doubt. Behind the pistol, his scruffy beard makes him look crazed. As he comes closer, the grey hair peppered in with the dark becomes visible.

"Ok, on the ground, bellies down." He starts to pat them down, Chris first, next Mark, and stops when he gets to Evelyn. "I'm trusting you little girl. You best mind your Ps and Qs 'round me. We respect women, but I will put a round in your skull if I have to. So now, who was talking? Let's get to it." The man folds his arms after holstering his pistol.

Mark unclasps his hands and rises to his knees. "That was me, my name is Mark. This is Chris and she's my daughter, Evelyn."

"I'm Dexter. I would say nice to meet you but, well, these days it's not all peaches and cream. I don't want to hurt you so I'm GOING to walk out of here with your weapons and you will not follow me." Dexter leans down to gather up the tools of the trade for this zombie apocalypse. As he stands up, Sarge's rifle is pointed at Dexter's neck, just at the base of the skull. Sarge leans in so the cold steel touches Dexter. His salt and pepper hair stands on end.

"I'm going to have to disagree with that." Sarge smirks. "You ok?"

Mark stands as do the others, "Yes, we're fine. What do we do with him?" Sarge puts the muzzle back to Dexter's head, "No, we are not going to kill him." Mark puts his hand on the barrel.

"And why not?" Sarge looks at Mark. "Don't tell me it's because you like this guy that was about to rob you and leave you to die?"

"No, he didn't want to hurt us. He was just looking out for himself. He can shoot, and we could use another good shot with all that's going on out there." Mark reasons with Sarge.

"So, you want us to take in this albeit good shot, possibly homicidal, thief? Right, that makes a ton of sense." Sarge says sarcastically

Chris chimes in, "Mark is right. Let's at least find out who he is and what he knows."

"Ok Ex, if you trust him, I do too. Not! Oh God, I've been around that little girl too long." Sarge shakes his head looking at Evelyn.

Evelyn looks at him, "Hey, I'm right here. I don't even say that. That was all you." Evelyn walks back to get the stack of linens.

"Well, you are out voted; we will talk to him." Mark pulls Dexter to his feet.

The group walks over to a table. Dexter is sitting across from Chris and Mark, Sarge is sitting on a table behind Dexter with one leg hanging off and his rifle at the ready. Joey walks to help Evelyn load up a rolling cart with 2x4s and the bags she had gotten.

"Tell us how you've made it out here alone this long." Mark opens a bottle of water and takes a drink.

"Well, I have been on the road for about two months now. Traveling town to town, finding what I can where I can." Dexter seems agitated by Sarge sitting behind him.

Chris picks up Mark's bottle, wipes the opening, and takes a sip. Sarge nods and smiles at Chris. "So, you have a car? Or a camp close by?"

Dexter looks at the bottle of water. As he answers, he doesn't take his eyes off it, "I just got into town today; haven't had time. I was going to find a place in here to dig in and stay the night."

"Did you have a group? Why are you alone?" Mark asks as though he were conducting a job interview.

"Um, well, I guess you could call it a group, but that's over… long over." A sad tone now washes over Dexter.

This pauses the brain trust of Mark, Chris and Sarge. "So, what does that mean?" Sarge speaks up.

"Just like you people I imagine, I've lost people close to me." Anger is now evident across Dexter's face.

"Calm down there Sparky." Sarge adjusts his weapon and stands, he has the Sarge super-power face and has tuned into something.

"What do you know about how this all started?" Chris tries to get back on track.

"I just know what I heard or saw. It all started kind of slow, a sick person here and there, but when it got crazy the news said, 'stay indoors and lock your home.' Next thing I knew, was my friend Cory was eating his wife on their front lawn… and not in a fun way."

"So, what else do you know? You said you've been on the road, right? What have you seen out there?" Chris is growing skeptical of Dexter's story.

"I haven't seen that much really. Most towns are like this one, a few of the Mooks here and there. Nothing like the first few weeks even months." Dexter licks his lips still eyeballing the water.

Mark gets up from the table and scans the common area for Evelyn and Joey. "So how many people were in your group? How'd you lose them?"

"People ain't made for this world; not the way it is now." He says sadly.

Sarge chuckles, "You got that right." Sarge takes Mark's seat across from Dexter, "You've handled this well. I take it this isn't your first rodeo. So, what are you, and what have you picked up from us?" Sarge now cuts to his blunt point.

"Ha-ha... you got me. Former DEA narcotics unit. I was a UC, worked deep cover. So yes, this isn't my first rodeo." Dexter now looks Sarge in the eyes. He is far more comfortable now. Stronger voice and speaking more clearly, almost losing his accent all together.

"How do you do that?" Chris is in awe of the Sarge's superpower.

"So now that you cut the bullshit, let's hear it." Sarge leans back in the chair as though he isn't intrigued.

"What I can tell is you all have been together for a while, maybe from the beginning. You're the boss, or at least you make play you are. You want me to think you have limited supplies by drinking from the same bottle of water. I think that 'bout sums it up?" Dexter smiles, proud of himself.

"Close. So how did you get out of the firebombing?" Mark rejoins the conversation.

"I didn't." Dexter lifts his shirt and all down his side are burn scars. Also, just above his pant line the name Hunter is tattooed. "It was a miscalculation on my part."

Sarge taking notice to the tattoo asks, "Who's Hunter?"

"A ghost…" Dexter looks at the ground.

Angel comes over the radio, "You guys have incoming."

"How many?" Chis responds.

"Ten, maybe fifteen; I don't know where they are coming from." Panic in her voice.

"Time to go. We have…" BANG! Before Chris can finish, the large caliber rifle can be felt inside.

"Guess there are more of you than I thought? Was that a 50-cal?" The stranger prods, with surprise in his voice scanning the group with his eyes.

"Dexter, I guess you'll fit in till the real enemy isn't around." Mark says, gathering up the gear and putting it in the duffel bag.

"Mark, the real enemy is always around." Dexter responds.

The sound of moans and gun fire gets more intense the closer they get to the doors. Each prepares for a fight but hopes for the best. The front doors open slowly as they radio to Angel they are coming out. The sun is still high in the cloudless sky but provides little warmth. The fifteen that had been quoted earlier was a gross underestimation. The sight of thirty rotting corpses litters the fenced in parking lot. More are emerging from the back side of the hotel, almost as if a movie or concert has just let out. Manny made his way to a scaffolding. The onslaught of mindless killers is too spread out to outrun and too vast to shoot a way through. A few have noticed the group of survivors and now are seeing their next meal. Chris uses the butt of the shotgun to smash in the closest one's skull.

"We need to move, NOW!" Sarge clicks into command mode.

The group closes the doors. Arms and faces try to prevent the door from shutting all the way. This is no longer a simple run, but now a very real threat. Evelyn and Joey push the cart to the side and forget the bounty they'd just gathered. Even Sarge is overwhelmed. The light that had been coming from the end of the hallway is flickering like a strobe light as the number of the dead walking intermittently interrupts it.

"Ok, we need to find a way to the trucks. Leave the supplies and let's go." Mark supersedes Sarge.

"Ev, stay close to me." Chris grabs her hand. "What way do we go, boss?" Chris looks at Mark.

"We need to find out what looks best from the outside." Mark keys his mic, "Angel, we need your eyes. What's the best route out of here? What's it looking like out there?"

"Mark, not good... You'll have a small window if you go to the north side doors." Angel reports

Mark looks down the north hall back the way they came, the light is still flickering, "You sure about that? It looks packed from here."

"Mark, trust me. I will get you all out of there." Angel sounds to be on the move.

Dexter looks around at the hodgepodge group, "Who are you talking to? How many people do you have out there? I hope it's a fucking army."

Sarge lands back on earth, "It's my daughter; she's out there… she's out there!" Sarge starts down the hall haphazardly.

"What's his deal? Did he say daughter? I hope she's got a cooler head than he does." Dexter is pulling his pistol.

"She's every bit of everything we need right now. She said she'd give us a window and I have faith she will." Mark pulls the proverbial boot-straps tight and starts down the hall, getting the group back to Sarge.

Angel comes over the radio, "Ok on ten you will have some time to move to the outside of the parking lot, those things haven't realized you aren't at the front anymore. You'll have to move fast. There's a big maybe 20-foot blue dumpster 'bout 15 yards to the west of the doors. If you can get there, I can open another window and get you out."

"Do we have a choice?" Mark replies. "Ok, big blue dumpster, that's where we're going. Give it everything you have to get there. She'll help us from there."

"Ok, Mark, we got this." Chris slings his shotgun over his back and looks Joey in the eyes, "Bet I'm faster."

Joey smiles and brushes his shoulder off, "Boys." Evelyn shakes her head.

"All joking aside, we need to be fast and tight. Sarge … Sarge! Are you with us?" Mark pushes Sarge.

"Yes, I'm here. I'm good." He looks at the line of Zeeks walking, taking a breath.

"I thought he was the strong one?" Dexter leans into Joey.

"He's deaf. He can't hear you." Evelyn informs Dexter.

"Ok Marine, ten count. one, two, three, four, five..." Sarge counts over the radio, finishing the count with his hands. The shots ring out with a thunderous thud. Blood sprays the windows of the door.

Soon after several shots have found their mark, Angel comes over the radio yelling "Go! Go! Go!"

The six run for their lives, the sunlight making visibility hard at first. The blue dumpster is in sight and only a few more strides away.

"Damn, she is a good shot." Dexter looks at the carnage left by just a few shots from the Angel of Death. Body parts and blood covering the ground. The asphalt glistening with that all too familiar thick, dark red, almost black blood.

The group makes it to their first check point. They move as to not be seen or draw unwanted attention to themselves. "Ok, you made it. Now you see the semi rig? On my shots, run to it." Angel commands. More loud and powerful shots rain down. This time the group has a front row seat to this bloody show. The air fills with a mist of blood. The few stragglers are now just a memory on the ground. The six of them move to the rig and hold there. They now have a line of sight to the trucks. However, almost 50 Zeeks stand between them and the way out.

"No way can she take out enough..." Chris surveys the area looking defeated.

"Angel save your rounds. That fifty is important. We're on our own from here." Mark says reluctantly but sounding more knowledgeable.

"But Mark, I can't just... I have to help you." Angel pleads.

"The tail end of that mob is already looking for where the sound came from. You need to get out of there while you still can." Mark has more care in his voice than panic.

"10-4. I better see you on this side of that gate." Angel answers.

Mark looks around, coming up with a plan, "So this is what's going to happen, you all will make a run for it to the trucks. I will lead them away. I will make it back to the hotel and hold up till they find something new to go after." Mark says with a strong voice.

"Dad, no, that's suicide!" Evelyn looks in her dad's weathered face.

"Ev keep your voice down. It's the only way..." Mark hugs his little girl for what may be the last time. He looks around one more time, pulls Chris in and grabs Sarge's hand, "It's your turn. Keep my little girl safe. Look after her as if she was your own." Sarge nods and shakes Mark's hand hard.

Mark turns to Dexter and Joey, "You better not turn out to be an asshole." Mark pulls the keys out of his pocket reaching out his hand, he looks up into Joey's sad eyes, "You take them, you give a man a chance now. Put him in your car and get him to safety. Just do it better and faster than I did." Mark smiles and tries to hand the keys to Joey.

Only Joey doesn't take them. Instead, he grabs Mark and hugs him good and tight before shoving him to the ground. Chris and Dexter realize what's about to happen at almost the same time.

"I know that look, he's about to do something stupid." Dexter looks around. It's as if time has slowed down.

Chris grasps for Joey, but knowing how Chris feels about him, Joey has already moved away. Joey signs, "Love you and see you later, my brother." Chris falls to his knees.

Joey takes off and the crowd starts to follow. His hands are waving, and his one-of-a-kind voice is louder than the Zeeks surrounding him.

Mark and Evelyn grab Chris, pulling him to his feet. Dragging him, he is facing the crowd and can see Joey making his way toward the hotel. He sees Joey fall. The group hears shots before everything goes silent...

 # Wayward Sons

The group has driven just a few hundred yards away; Mark stops to jump out. Trying to see or hear anything to confirm Joey is alive. He stands for what feels like hours but was far less. He hangs his head and climbs back into his SUV. One friend, one family member short. The heavy feeling in the vehicle seems as though they are deep under the ocean, every part of them feeling this loss. Mark hasn't looked in the rearview mirror once. The fear he'd turn back is too great, and he realizes he must keep those still in his company alive. A task that is becoming more and more taxing.

The sound of the tires change from the whir of two-lane roadway to a steady thumping on hard packed dirt, the mood becomes a little bit lighter. They know they are almost home, and after what happened they can't take home for granted. Mark is bringing up the rear of the convoy, when suddenly the big black truck stops. Dust flies and in the cloud, Mark is snapped back to reality. Sarge steps out and Angel does as well. They have stopped just a few miles away from the cabin. Mark climbs out.

"What's up? Why'd you stop?" Mark asks while waving the cloud of dust away dramatically.

"We don't know this guy, but he is clearly trained. If it was me, I'd have been tracking and logging where we were going, so I'd know how to get back when I slipped out. Now, don't get me wrong, I'm a sweet, kind-hearted neighbor, but do we really want this guy to know exactly where we live?" Sarge brings up a good point in his own brand of speaking.

"I feel you, but do we have time to go anywhere else right now?" Mark points up at the sun dropping below the trees.

"You tell me. He's your charge." Sarge looks at Manny in the back of the truck, "I have this one you take that one."

"Hey Sarge, we've come too far now. He knows most of the way, I say we just push to the cabins and tell him we'll go back in the morning and then he can go wherever." Angel pipes out, getting back into the truck.

"Sounds good to me." Mark starts back to his truck leaving Sarge no choice and standing alone.

The trucks start on their way again, Dexter in Mark's, seemingly calm and supportive. "I know that was about me and, I can tell by the way you all took that kids death just now I know you aren't out to hurt or steal anything, so you have no worries from me. Just give me a bed for the night and a ride back to the main road in the morning and we are even." Dexter sounds sincere.

"Even? Even for what?" Chris asks gingerly.

"Me telling you what really happened." Dexter is covered in seriousness.

Before they get any further, the trucks pull up on the cabins. Dexter is almost in shock at the twelve cabins in near perfect condition, how the lake seems clean, and the windmill easily spinning in the light breeze. The two crews become one as they spill out of the cabins and climb down out of the trucks. Kids running to parents and smiles that can't be fought off. It quickly becomes evident someone is missing.

Elsa looks around "Manny, where's Joey?" She questions as she hugs him.

Ryan is also quick to realize his big brother-like friend isn't around, "Dad... where's... Jo-." He starts as tears fill his little eyes realizing quickly the way the dark world works.

Mark kneels and wraps his loving arms around Ryan. Evelyn drops on top of them as Mark tells his son that Joey won't be coming home. Mark stands and looks up to see all eyes are on him now. His face full of pain, taking on a role he never asked for nor wanted. However, he has found himself in it now.

"Ok guys, yes, we lost one of ours today, but he went out as a hero..." Mark chokes up.

Evelyn puts her hand on his arm, "But we wouldn't be here if it wasn't for him. He saved us and now we have to keep living for him."

Mark collects himself, "He wanted us to know he was useful and that he wasn't the weak link. He never was. But like Ev said, we wouldn't be here without him, including this man. Mark points at Dexter who has been on the outside of the circle, "This is Dexter, we found him at the hotel."

Sarge butts in, "And that reminds me, we never finished our cutting-through-the-bullshit talk. Let's go do that."

Mark, a little unhappy he didn't get to finish honoring Joey, agrees. Sarge leads Dexter to a less-used cabin, one with less than standard living conditions. It has an old rickety table and chairs out front. The screen door is hanging on by one hinge, and its windows are mostly missing. The kids would take turns seeing who could walk the furthest up the creaky wooden steps before the ghost they'd created got them. These men aren't worried one bit by the ghosts of fiction as all of them seem to be haunted by much more real problems.

Now that the reformed interrogation squad has sat down, Sarge waves Manny over. "What, you need me to go get your ashtray?" Manny snaps.

"No, sit, we need to talk to this guy." Sarge cuts a don't-you-say-another-word look at Manny.

Now, Dexter is more willing to speak openly. He tells them how he'd driven to the hotel for the same reasons. How he had found some food still in boxes like they were preparing for a grand opening. After he tells them how his car was parked a few blocks away and how he'd scouted the hotel for a few days, he lets them know why he was so eager to shoot on sight.

"Much like everywhere, some folks just want to take-food, supplies, women, life... Now, I'm almost positive you had to have run into this at least once before. There is a group out there. Full of some backwoods, nasty sons-a-bitches. They look like maybe they were militia, or something like that, before all this. Who knows what or who they think they are fighting for. All I know is, if you have it, they want it. They don't care if you live or die, they don't want to save or help anyone but their own." He shifts in the flimsy lawn chair.

"So, where are they?" Mark asks

"I don't know exactly but I know where they tend to be."

"Well, I say we steer clear of that place." Manny giggles.

Sarge shakes his head and resets the conversation, "Now, what is it you're looking for? Who was this group you were with and was it them who ended that partnership?"

Reluctantly, Dexter shares more of the story, "My group... It was my family. My wife and son. My boy, 5 years old, and my poor wife." He starts to crumble in his chair, "I couldn't save them and that's on me, we should have just left when she told me to." A seriousness in his voice.

Chris is hit hard by Dexter's words "Hunter? That's who Hunter is?"

"Yeah, that's my boy. Was my boy... When this all started, he had just finished kindergarten. We were outside having a graduation for him. My wife was a teacher back in L.A. but when we moved here and had him, she decided to home school him. We lived on a farm, not that I know how to run one, but after L.A. we just wanted open spaces and quiet." He smiles at the memory.

"So, what happened?" Mark prods feeling a parallel to this story.

Dexter suddenly seems angry and sits up in his chair moving closer to the table, "It was when they burned the cities; we went out to see who or what we could find. Only the fires must have flushed them out, too. First, my senses told me we were ok, but then I felt like we were being watched. As we walked back to the car, I noticed things out of place from before. I went to put my son in the car and when I looked up, guys were coming out of the burnt-out buildings. I didn't want to stick around to find out what they wanted. As I looked in the mirror to see if they'd started following us, I found to my surprise they hadn't. We got back to the farm and that's when she told me maybe we should have left. Weeks after we argued again. She said it wasn't going to be like when the fires broke out and I just had to see what was going on. She knew I'd make any fight my fight or if someone was in danger, I'd help..." He looks around and clams up.

"So, what happened then?" Angel walking in, encourages him to continue as she stops beside Mark.

Dexter's eyes go blank playing a memory in his head, "That's not what I'm here to talk about. I can tell you a few places that may help out a group this size, but in the morning if you don't mind. I want to get some rest." Dexter stands up, awaiting a dismissal. Sarge agrees and points at the most rundown cabin indicating this is his holding cell. After Dexter makes his way into the cabin, Sarge reveals what he took away from the story.

"This guy knows a lot more than he's telling us. For starters, he said cities-not city. If he had no contact with anyone, how'd he know they firebombed more than one? I'm also not sure he is who he says he is. Maybe he was a cop, but no way am I buying the rest." Sarge gets up and looks at Manny, "As for you, this guy is a wild card so we can't let him think we aren't all on the same page. I still don't trust you, but for now I trust you more than him. Angel, you set up a watch schedule. Someone will be posted here all night and make sure he knows it."

Later in the night, as the first watch comes to an end, Mark and Angel start to talk about life before. Mark lays back on the picnic table, looking up at the stars, feeling the chill in the night air enter his lungs. "So, what did you want to be when you grew up? Or was the goal always to be a sniper?" Mark nudges Angel who's sitting on the bench to his left facing the cabins.

"Wow, you know, I never really think about that anymore. I've done this for so long, I couldn't see myself as anything else." Angel takes in a deep breath, looking up at the stars herself.

"It's hard for me to look up at a star-filled night and not think about all the 'what could have been' you know? The stars remind me of being a kid with everything yet to be decided." Mark sits up, peering out into the dark woods, then down at Angel. This late in the year nature is still and silent.

She turns to look up at him, "I guess I wanted to be a soccer player."

Mark floored, shakes his head as if it would change what he heard. Sliding off the table and sitting on the bench next to her he feels his heart beat slow to a more normal pace. He's grown accustomed to always being on edge, staying there because it could be the difference between life and death.

"A soccer player? I did not see that coming." Mark looks towards her. She's still looking up.

"Yes, why does that shock you? I loved it actually. I started in middle school and I was good. We went to state twice in high school and won it once." She sighs and looks at the ground, "My dad was always gone in those days, so my brother or host of Marine wives turned care takers, would come to my games. That seems like a lifetime ago. Thinking about it now, I feel it was the only time I felt free in my life." Angel looks at Mark and then at the cabin, "Gee, thanks for bringing me down, jerk." She leans over and bumps Mark with her shoulder.

Mark smiles and nods in acceptance, "Not my plan. Being up here, looking at the sky, reminds me of when I was young and dumb just trying to make the world a better place."

"Well, it's not too late. You may not be young, but you're still pretty dumb." She jokes with him.

"Oh snap! I see how it is." Mark stands up in front of Angel, her blond hair glowing even in the dark of the night. Finding it hard not to smile looking down at her. She kicks dirt at his boot.

"Mark, can I ask you something? Don't let me babble or anything. I just need to know something. I'm bad with people stuff. I think even when I was young, too. Not having a mom to show me and all that, and my dad wasn't the best example. Even still, I just have to figure something out..." Mark kicks her to end the running around in her mind. "So, you, me, this? Am I that far off or...?"

"Hey guys." Evelyn's voice pops the bubble Mark and Angel were in.

"Ev, hey, is it time already?" Now completely back to reality, Mark looks into Evelyn's eyes seeing his sweet girl and, at the same time, Rachel.

"Dad?" She can see something is off and directs her confusion to Angel who all but put a bag over her head to hide from the situation. "Is everything ok here?"

Angel stands and grabs her rifle, "Yes, Mark just asked what I wanted to be when I grew up and he didn't believe me when I said a fairytale princess." Angel walks off into the night, making noise at first but soon vanishes.

"Maybe a wicked stepmom." Evelyn jokes.

Chris looks at Mark trying not to make the obvious joke because it would be too nail-on-the-head. "What's with everyone tonight? Y'all are acting weird."

Mark puts his hand on Chris's shoulder, then hugs Evelyn "Good night you two, don't get too distracted."

Leaving them, Mark returns to his room, kicks off his boots, and falls into bed. Sleep is far off as his mind is on the direction Angel was going. Rachel on his mind like always. Thinking to himself: *Rach, I still love you. I can't be feeling this for her. It's too soon, and Ev and Ryan would hate me. I know you said I'd have to move on and try and find happy, but I don't know that I can or that I want to find happy in someone else's arms...*

Mark's face is warmed by the sun peeking through the window. The days are getting colder now, and the sun feels good, like the warm hand of a loved one telling him everything is ok and gently touching his cheek to make it so. The sound of wood being chopped pulls him from his slumber. Slowly he moves to the mirror hanging on the wall, a few pictures taped to it. One of the kids playing in the water, another of the family in the car on a trip up to the lake, and one that sits about eye level to Mark. This one is of Rachel. He had taken it while she was asleep. He'd joked with her about it being his favorite because she was asleep and wasn't being a smart ass or didn't have some prank or joke planned. It is just her as she was, wavy, messy blonde bed hair, blankets covering her lower half just below her lower back, slightly tanned skin like the sun had just kissed her. The lower half that's being covered looks like a beautiful mountain range that rises and falls with all her curves.

After a long look at it, Mark pulls it down and puts it in the pocket of his pants, "I need you with me; I can't do any of this alone anymore."

Outside now, Mark sees Meg pacing, Elsa ushering the kids off, and Manny yelling at Sarge. As he gets closer, he can make out the words. Something about a glow in the woods and how they can't trust this new guy. Mark looks to Chris for the update on what happened, a cup of coffee in Chris's hand, knuckles white as he grips it tight. He looks worn out and worried.

Mark looks for Evelyn. She's nowhere to be seen and he feels the worry start to build. His steps get slower as he walks up to the fire pit. "Hey, Hey, Hey, what's going on? Why is everyone so aggravated?" He asks.

Sarge rolls his eyes a bit, "Ex and Evelyn saw a glow in the woods last night and now Manny thinks we are all going to die." Smirk on his face.

"Dude, that's not what I said. I said, if that guy has people out there, and now they know where we are, how safe are we?" Manny has a different level of confidence in his voice than when he's spoken to Sarge in the past.

"What kind of glow?" Mark looks to Chris for clarification.

Chris hands Mark the coffee and starts to explain the events of their watch. "So Ev and I were talking about Joey when she heard something in the woods, maybe sixty yards out or so. I got up to walk that way when a glimpse of a green glow moved behind the trees. I stopped and, thinking it was someone coming for our new friend, I returned to watch his cabin. I'm thinking, must have just been our minds playing tricks."

Remembering Angel walked out that way, Mark points out that maybe it was her doing what she does. They realize they haven't seen her yet this morning. As they discuss other possibilities, Sarge asks Mark to check on Dexter.

"So, you go wake up your new charity case!" The grizzled man barks.

"I don't understand why you still do that after all this time. We aren't your troops and I'm sure as shit not a kid." Mark, the smaller man, takes a step in Sarge's direction.

"Just go before I really get mad. Besides, you don't have the balls to do anything about it anyway." Sarge walks past Mark, slamming his shoulder into Mark's.

"I've had it!" Mark launches the coffee cup, hot coffee and all, at Sarge's back.

Sarge lets out a quick but brawny yelp, "You son of a bitch!" Sarge turns and marches toward Mark staring down at him in his patented look. The Marine takes a step back.

Meg takes a breath, "Thank yo..." Before she can finish her sentence, Sarge swings and cracks Mark across the jaw, sending him hurtling to the ground.

"There, bitch! Stay down there or I'll put you flat on your ass again." Proud of himself, the tough guy turns his back.

Mark has truly had enough; not heeding the warning given, he stands, the anger building inside him. Rage, loss, grief, and frustration within himself, spill over like a boiling pot. Before the group can do anything, Mark springs at Sarge like he was shot out of a gun. Mark wraps one arm around Sarge's neck and tightens the hold by lacing the other behind his head and squeezing with all the strength he can muster.

Rage is bridging the gap between skill and will; Sarge drops to his knees. A quick elbow to Mark's ribs causing him to loosen his grip around Sarge's neck. Using this new space, he tucks his chin and delivers another well-placed elbow. With a meaty thud Mark has no choice but to let go. Reeling from the hard-pinpoint shots to the ribs, Mark has one arm tucked tightly against his abdomen. Without his guard up, Sarge lands a solid uppercut, catching Mark squarely on the chin...

September 11, 2001

The sound of sneaky shuffling wakes Mark up. He looks at the clock, it's 7:14 am.

"What's going on?" Mark asks groggily

Rachel, seeing him roll over in the bed to look at her, smiles and takes a few quick steps and flops down on the bed with a big grin, "I just got some big news and I'm too excited!"

Mark, still in the shallow reach of sleep, isn't ready for the ball of energy Rachel is even after all this time together, "Oh yeah? What is it?" He asks eye lids squinted and heavy.

Rachel reaches into her back pocket, slides out a pregnancy test, and puts it in front of his still sleepy eyes, "Remember that time when Ev wanted to sleep outside one last time before school started? You and I had the house to ourselves and... You know?" She now has and even bigger grin.

"WHAT?" Mark, now fully awake and taking in this beautiful moment, "No way! Are you sure?" He asks with a now equal level of excitement in him.

"As sure as peeing on a stick. I have a doctor appointment later today to find out for sure." She wraps her arms around him in the most loving embrace a husband and wife can share. Creating a life and doing so with your soulmate is the ultimate joy.

"Rach, the test?" Mark says lips still pressed to hers.

"What about it?" She responds, eyes closed.

"It's touching me. You peed on it." His eyes glued to the home pregnancy test now against his cheek.

She releases her hug. Laughing she says, "Oh sorry. It's ok, your breath is terrible anyway."

Now downstairs in the kitchen, Mark turns on the tv. Rachel is pouring a bowl of cereal, and Mark calls to her, pointing at the tv. Not ready for what she sees on screen the bowl hits the ground. A plane has just struck the North Tower of The World Trade Center. The happy is sucked from them faster than it infected them earlier. The voice on tv says, "We still aren't sure if this was an accident or intentional."

"Babe, what's going on? How could that happen?" Rachel, still frozen in place speaks out.

"I'm not sure. I don't know how that could be an accident..." Mark states bleakly.

They move about the house like ghosts, catching bits of the news coverage. "Oh my GOD!" Mark hears from the next room. He rushes in to see the aftermath of a second plane having just flown into the South Tower. Floored once more, tears fall from their eyes striking the ground.

The clock reads 9:20AM and they must leave to go to the doctor appointment, trying to keep some joy in the day. On the drive there is no music, just talk of what could be going on and how reports are still coming in. They pull into the parking lot, just before they get out of the car the voice on the radio continues, sadness reverberating through the speakers, "We have just learned another plane has just collided with the Pentagon in Washington, D.C. I still do not understand who could do such a thing... as soon as we know more, we will report it."

Sitting in the examination room, Mark puts his thoughts into words, "We should take self-defense classes."

Giggling, "You, in a fight? Sorry to laugh."

"No, seriously, we should at least know some basic stuff so if put in a situation we may be able to get away..." Mark insists.

"Wow, I never thought you'd say you wanted to learn to fight." Rachel smiles and finger waves him over.

"I'd do anything to protect you girls and my new baby boy." He goes in for the kiss.

Rachel pushes him away, "Boy? I thought you wanted girls?"

He overpowers her push and lands the kiss before she can pull away, "Yeah, but you want a boy. So, I got my girl, you should have your boy; we'll flip for the third."

She laughs, "I still can't get over you in a fight. I just keep picturing you standing like a 30s boxer."

Becoming annoyed, he sternly tells her, "One day, I will go toe-to-toe with the biggest, toughest guy you'll ever see, and although I may not win, I won't back down."

"Aww babe, I believe you." Rachel smiles sweetly at him.

KNOCK, KNOCK, "Doctor Watson." The door opens but instead of a person coming through it, a gush of water hits Mark square in the face.

Waking up from the KO punch, Mark looks up to see a hand reaching for him. His eyes focus and Sarge has his hand out. Mark grabs it. Helping him up to his feet, he pulls Mark in for a hug. Mark's bell still rung. He is unsure what is going on. "I'm sorry. I know you never asked for this and you are doing your best. I think I'm just mad at myself and taking it out on you Mark." Sarge confesses while still pulling him close.

Mark looks the humbled man in his eyes, "Same. Besides you just helped me keep a promise I made to Rachel."

Sarge seems confused but agrees that both are at fault. Before they part, Angel appears "Hey old man, is there something you need to tell me?"

The two men with ego to lose, let go of the embrace. The lady sniper and recon expert informs them of her most recent lap around. "So, I took a sweep last night and it was all clear, but this morning I noticed some tracks, a two-man team. Came in from the north side of the lake. I tracked them back to the foot paths, but the trail went cold. I'll take you all there."

"That will have to wait, I think we need to get this wildcard out of here first." Mark points at the cabin Dexter is in.

"That hit to the head turn you into me?" Sarge askes while hugging Meg.

"No, but no coincidence he gets here and now we have people in the woods. We've been here for months and nothing. He shows up, and people are, what did you say, sixty yards away?" Mark scans the group.

Angel realizing she's missed something, "Hit to the head? What happened?"

"I'll give you the rundown later, I agree with that though, he's out. Let's wake him up." Chris heads toward the cabin.

BOOM, BOOM, BOOM on the cabin door, "Dexter! Hey, come on out! Time to hit the road" Chris yells. As the door creeks open, Dexter is shirtless and walking away from the door. Chris notices a tattoo on his back, the image is of a woodpecker and the word 'Peckerwood' under it a few other tattoos scattered around his body, but in the dim cabin light are hard to make out. The tattoo is all too familiar to Chris who grew up in Texas. His voice as mean and accent as thick as it's ever been, Chris commands Dexter, "Get your shit so we can get you home." Chris storms down the steps and past the group without a word.

Meg, seeing this, "What's wrong with him?" She kisses Sarge on the lips and starts to walk after him, "I'll go find out, I guess. I feel like I'm still the office manager."

The door slams behind them. Dexter is standing on the porch, holding his bag and a bottle, "Can I get some water?" He walks as relaxed as can be. "Thanks for putting me up here last night. My place is a ways away, I can take you there and get you fixed up with some canned food. With just me there now, I won't need so much." Dexter looks at Manny "He looks like he eats a lot anyway."

"Hey buddy, you don't know me, don't say crap like that." Manny gripes.

As much as he doesn't want to, Sarge stands up for Manny, "Sorry, but he's my punching bag. How about a little respect?" Sarge gives the order to load up and move out. They take one truck, Sarge's. The men all get in the cab; Mark sits in back with Manny leaving Sarge and Dexter up front. They head out, Mark, who is behind Dexter, puts a round in the chamber. Click, Clack. Dexter looks in the side view mirror at Mark who is looking right back at him. As this rolling truck of awkward sets off, Dexter starts to hum.

Growing agitated, Mark hits the seat back, "Sorry. Hey Dexter, what were you looking for if you had so many supplies?"

"I had some of the dead mess up a barricade I set up, so I needed something to fix it. I knew that hotel would have construction equipment." Dexter shifts in his seat to look back.

The truck comes to a stop just outside the gated area of the hotel. Dexter jumps out "Let me grab my stuff out of my hiding spot and put it in back."

Manny calls out, "Didn't he say he had a car not a hiding spot?"

Dexter hops back in the truck. He directs them to his home. Mostly two-lane roads with grass on the sides, every so often Sarge goes off the road sliding the truck sideways in the grass. "Gotta have fun when you can. What's the point of a truck like this if you don't get it dirty, right?" Sarge grins, referring to his high horsepower and lifted off road truck.

After thirty minutes of driving on and off the road, they arrive at a blue farmhouse. Wrap around deck and a screened in porch off the back. The second story looks like its seen better days. The land it sits on is vast. At least the length of a football field in all directions before you hit any tree line. Sarge gets out and is instantly in love with the set up. There are big crop irrigation sprinklers tipped so the wheels face away from the house creating a barricade around the front of the house. They have barb wire laced through them. Beyond that, a trench dug about six feet deep that runs about two feet from the barricade. One path about three feet wide is laid leading to the front door, but it's protected by chain link like that from the hotel.

The house itself has standard railing on the front porch, only behind the spindles are thick metal plates. The windows are boarded up, but with small sections removed for eyes or guns. As they walk up to the gate, Dexter points at the ground, "Stay on the red dirt, the dark dirt is land mined. Oh, and don't touch anything metal past the trench, it's all electrified."

Sarge, blown away by this improvised strong hold, can't help but ask, "How long have you had this setup? This must have taken a long time by yourself."

Dexter pulls gloves out of a tree trunk next to the gate and opens it, "Rubber gloves to keep the 8,000 volts from lighting me up. I wasn't alone. We started working before all of this."

"Jesus, 8,000 volts?" Manny asks, jaw on the ground.

"Yes sir. I know it sounds like a lot but really all it is, is a bear fence hooked into all of this, like they use in Alaska to keep bears off property. It's enough to back you up if you bump it." Dexter boasts.

"That's enough to kill you." Mark walks through the gate.

Inside, they see a full-on cross between if grandma and an armory got to decorate. Guns at every window and ammo at

Crop Irrigation System = fence
HOUSE

the ready. In the front room, the sofa looks and smells like it has been in the room since the 1960s the only new things in the room are a few tv monitors. Past the front room is a kitchen; a stove is the only appliance that belongs. A few shelves with canned food and MREs line the wall between the two rooms. In the dining room, it looks like a hospital, plastic covers the walls and instead of a chandelier, a medical light hangs over a rolling EMT stretcher. On the wall farthest from the window that is covered by a steel plate, is a hutch full of medicines and other medical supplies.

"Man, you have what scares and excites me all in one house." Mark enviously looking room to room.

Sarge, too, is looking around but for very different reasons, "I see the one way in and a way out the back? Only two doors to cover."

"Yep. I don't use the upstairs, and the back porch is my fall back. I know this is a lot, but after what I saw in my life, I wanted to be ready for anything. Some people are savages even back before." A guarded Dexter replies.

"That you are." Manny agrees, looking at a picture on the wall. He takes a longer look at the picture of Dexter and several men. He wipes the dust off the glass.

"Don't touch stuff, please. I was polite and stayed in that run-down cabin, so respect my home." Dexter puts his bag down on a table in the front room. "I'm going to go hit the switch for the genny. It's dark in here." Dexter unlocks a door off the kitchen and closes it behind him. This door is heavy and made of steel, like something you'd see in a hospital.

Sarge, wasting no time, grabs the bag Dexter put down looking inside. Some clothes and a few stray bullets, "Mark, I think we just walked into the last place we'll ever walk into."

"What?" Mark steps into the front room.

Sarge dumps the bag out. Landing on the table is a swastika bandana and a map with the lake circled. "I think he was looking for us."

"We have guns and there's only one of him." Mark declares.

"I don't think he's alone" Manny says, looking out one of the slots in the window, "A few dudes just pulled up."

"That's right, my boys are here now. I'm going to need you to drop your weapons." Dexter emerges from the locked room.

"So how long have you been watching us?" Sarge inquires, setting his rifle on the ground.

"Shit, we wasn't watching you. Like I said, I needed to fix the barricade out back and just happened on y'all." Dexter motions with his gun for the three of them to move away from the door.

"So why was the lake marked on the map?" Mark points at the map on the table.

Dexter moves to look at the map, "Oh that? We was just trying to find more places to set up and we knew the cabins were up there."

"So why wait to bring us here if you had men outside our camp last night?" Manny speaks.

"What are you talking 'bout? We didn't care about you. The fellas were a day's drive away." Dexter replies defensively.

Sarge kicks Manny's foot telling him to shut up. "Now, I'm going to ask you not to speak again in my house, Mexican. I've taken about as much as I can of you, and when they get in here, if I've already popped you, I don't get my reward."

"So, was your family ever real?" Mark wondering if he just played on his heart strings.

"Yeah, they was real, till my old lady wanted me to start helping the other races. 'Take them in' she said. 'they are people too', she said. With all them dead walking out there, I figured it was our lord GOD solving the problem. Hell, I wasn't going to hurt y'all till I saw this Mexi pile of shit sitting there." Dexter opens the door, two overweight men. "Look Ian, I got you some race traitors and a piñata." Dexter seems pleased with himself.

"Would you look at that?" Ian says, his belly hanging out from his shirt, SS and other white supremacist tattoos covering his arms and neck. "Now see here, that's why we come up this way. You always have something nice for us. They up in them cabins you told us about?" A thick drawl in his voice.

"Yes sir." Dexter has a big grin.

"This all of them?" The other man asks. He has tattoos for hair and eyebrows. The tattoos on his eyebrows reads Pecker, and the other Wood. This man is not very tall but is also overweight.

"No, that's the best part. They got at least three women, maybe a few kids. One other guy too." Dexter looks as if he's the goose that lays golden eggs.

"Why, that is nice." The man with the tattooed face walks closer. "Now, I don't have all day, but to let you know the shit you're in right now, you stand accused of treason to your race, and trespassing. How do you plead?"

Sarge doesn't speak, just stares into the man's eyes. Mark looks at the ground, unsure what to do. Manny starts to speak when Ian cuts him off, "Shut up, bitch, you don't get out of this vertical. Bet you hopped the fence."

The man with the face tattoos is still looking at Sarge who stands six inches or so taller "You got something to say?" He barks.

In the most-calm voice Sarge replies, "So you were a cop?" He turns his gaze to Dexter.

"Yeah, I was. I was a UC. I was told to go undercover and get close to a group of white supremacists. When I started, I was surprised to hear what they had to say, and they spoke to my soul." Dexter sounds as though he's preaching.

"Then what?" Sarge asks.

"Then, I realized I was there for a reason. After what I seen cartels and gangs do to each other I knew it was us against them. So, when I had a meet with my lead investigator, I shot his black ass." He says with a proud conviction in his voice.

"He became one of us for good." Tattoo face grins. Sarge starts to laugh, "Something funny to you?" Tattoo face barks.

That all too familiar Sarge smirk appears "I just can't take you seriously with those eyebrows." Sarge stops smiling.

"Is that right?" The man takes another step closer and puts a gun barrel to Sarge's gut, "Still funny?" Before the man realized what happened, Sarge has sunk a knife in the man's lung from the side. Now the fight is on.

Sarge pushes the almost lifeless man's body toward Dexter who was trying to take aim at him. Ian hasn't even cleared his holster by the time Sarge is on him. Dexter is pinned under the dead weight, Manny and Mark are going for the door. Thwack, Thwack, Thwack. Bullets ricochet off the door frame sending wood splinters flying. Sarge, straddles the large man who is unconscious after the beating Sarge has laid upon him. Mark has picked up Sarge's gun and nudges him with it, snapping him back to reality.

"Move! Back door, now! Move!" Sarge yells.

Manny is the first out the door. Dexter is still pinned. Mark is right behind Manny, Sarge turning to cover their exit is out the door last. Manny starts out the porch door when Mark grabs him.

"What? We need to go." Manny shrugs Mark off.

"Land mines and who knows what else is out that door, remember?" Mark calms them.

"Shit, you're right Mark." Sarge looks around the screened in porch realizing this is the worst place to stop, "Back inside now."

Dexter is up and coming right at them. Mark halts him with a straight hand to the nose. Dexter flat on his back, Sarge puts the muzzle of the gun to his face, "Smile and wait for the flash." Sarge leans in.

Manny stops him, "Wait, he knows the way out of here."

"Damnit you're right." Sarge pulls back, "Up. Now."

"Why would I help you?" Dexter wipes the blood from his nose.

"Because, unlike you, bullets don't discriminate." Mark points toward the gunfire.

"I know you have a way out the back, take us to it now!" Sarge barks louder than the gunfire out front.

Dexter starts to walk, "Out back! They're going out the bac..." Dexter gets a hit to the back of the head.

"We just need to get to where they can see us." Sarge pushes Dexter forward.

"Why do we want the people shooting at us to see us?" Manny asks.

 "Not them, Angel." Sarge says, still pushing Dexter

"Why? She's miles away." Mark says staying close to Sarge.

 "Did you really think I was having fun before? I was leaving fresh tracks to follow in case this was a trap." Sarge reveals, "Dexter, where from here?" Sarge questions as they come to the edge of the barricade looking around for cover.

 The gunshots have stopped, "They'll be on us now; we need cover." Sarge gestures to an old car to their left. "Target the door."

"Why didn't we stay inside?" Manny ducks down.

 "I didn't know if it was wired and I like not being blown up. Besides I can't signal for help from in there. Angel needs to see us so I can call the shots." Sarge perches his rifle on the hood of the car.

 Dexter points to their rear, "Bullets from the front, them dead things to the rear. What'cha going to do now?"

 The sound of gunfire has brought the unbiased enemy. As they stumble and drag to them, it suddenly dawns on them the back barricade was breached. No sooner than they remember, the dead are too close. "Zeeks. Six o'clock! Mark, cover the door! Manny here!" Sarge hands Manny a gun he had hidden on his ankle. "You and me clear the Zeeks. Mark, you got the door."

 Pop, Pop, Pop, Pop. Bang, Bang. The dead start to drop; some move faster at them. Dexter sees his moment to get away; he takes off running around the side of the house. Sarge yells to let him go. They need Mark to keep an eye on the door. More and more are spilling through the opening.

 "Where are they coming from?" Mark asks, looking around the wide-open space.

"Ten yards past the barricade. Looks like out of the ground." Sarge yells.

They look to see what he's talking about. Manny makes a startling discovery. The dead that now all but surround them are all minorities. "They let them turn, didn't killed them."

 "I guess that's what he meant by 'solving the problem'. Slaves. They kept them as some kind of an army." Sarge deduces. "Fall back to the house, there's too many!" He yells

"The house? Is it safe?" Mark starts that direction.

 "Safer than out here, I hope!" Exclaims Manny who is also running that way.

 "I'd bet they are long gone by now. They knew this was here and we'd end up food. I bet that's why they never moved in on us." Sarge gets to the door first, clears the kitchen, and waves the others in. "Ok boys, this is thick, and till we can signal for help, it's on us. Manny, you cover the back door. Mark, you cover the front. I'm going to try and get into the locked room. I bet all the fun toys are in there."

 They break off to the front, back, and locked door. Sarge tries to kick the door a few times, then takes a closer look, realizing short of some explosives, there is no way in without the keys and possibly the PIN to the keypad on the handle. As Sarge starts to make a plan, Mark calls out, "This guy is waking up in here!"

Sarge forgot that the second of the two men just got beaten to within an inch of his life wasn't all the way lifeless. "Good, he may have a key. Manny, how we looking on time?"

"We have maybe 80 to 90 of those things out there now. That screen ain't going to hold long then they're at our door." Manny growing frantic, calls back.

"Roger that!" Sarge moves quickly to the bloody heap of a man on the floor in the front room. "Ok jack off, you're going to get me into that room or you're going out to the poor saps you let get that way."

The man gurgles and gargles on blood and maybe teeth. Mark steps back to Sarge, "They are getting around front. I see maybe 30 out there now. You think these traps and stuff are the real deal..." Before Mark can finish, BOOM! Chunks of Zeek hit the house, "Well, that answers that."

Sarge gets the large man up and to the locked door, "Open it, or I feed you to the mob outside."

Still sloppy, "You just going to kill me anyway." The man coughs out.

"Yeah, but think of it this way, this old white boy does it quick or all them fine people of color out there do. Wait, do you all believe in that whole 70 virgins thing? I get all you bastards mixed up."

The man still refuses to help, so Sarge manhandles him to the porch and the view they're met with is of more Zeeks than can be counted, all surrounding the porch. Sarge closes the door and the man, terrified, runs back to it, begging to be let in. A sickening ripping noise, louder than the man's pleas to be let in can be heard behind him. They have broken down the screen The fear is becoming dread.

"Ok! Ok! I'll open it! Just let me in!" They open the door for him, he heads right to the door puts in a code, and the door unlocks.

On the other side of the door, it looks like a different world than the rest of the house, well lit, clean, and computers with several monitors. It has the look of what was a bathroom, all but the tile has been removed. On the desk, a keyboard and a few levers and switches are centered. Sarge sits in the rolling chair and looks up at the monitors. Seeing camera feeds from around the house. He looks at the monitor on the desk; it has file folders and a tab marked "counter measures." He clicks it. More tabs pop up these are labeled "Front door" "back door" "water" and "final". He looks at the out of breath man on the ground in the doorway, "What do these do?" He asks.

"The "back door" will bring down the roof of the porch blocking off the door. The "front door" will bring down the deck out front so nothing can get to the door. "Final" will blow the entire house. That guy was a lunatic. He had the entire thing set up well before this shit happened." He explains.

"What does "water" do?" Sarge turns in his chair.

"I don't know, it's new. I've never seen that one." The man huffs.

Sarge clicks the tab. It pulls up a small window on the front of the house and the barricade. Also, a gauge for water level. Unsure what's about to happen, he calls to Mark, telling him to stand back from the door. A count down timer appears in the gauge. 3, 2, 1, Initiate. The sprinklers start to spray the Zeeks out front, and its no small amount of water. With the ground now covered in water for 35 feet, the Zeeks as well, the idea clicks for Sarge. Watching the monitor, Sarge realizes the 8,000 volts are now going into everything the water touches. Every

Zeek out front is dropping or shaking violently; some close to the barricade are even catching fire.

"Mark, what's it look like out there?" Sarge yells.

"It worked! It's all clear up here, but if what I think just happened, how do we know the ground is safe to walk on?" Mark answers.

 "Hey, how do you shut down the barricade power?" Sarge looks back, the man is in and out of awareness. Sarge claps his hands, "Hey Ian! It's Ian, right?"

 "What, Yeah." He snaps back.

"How-do-you-shut-down the power?" Sarge slows it down.

"Press F7 then the S key." Ian mumbles.

 Sarge does and a new tab comes up with on/off sliders for all the systems. He finds the one marked "barricade" and turns it off. "Good to go." He jumps out of the chair and looks down at Ian "Get up. You're coming with us." He pulls Ian up off the ground and drags him to the front. "Manny let's go. Get your ass moving."

 They run to the truck without regard for the land mines. Once there, Sarge grabs a black bag out from under his seat; conveniently, it has rope inside. He looks at Ian and instructs him to put out his hands. Once tied up, Sarge puts the bag over his head puts him in the back seat.

"We're taking hostages now?" Mark seems displeased.

 "Look, I know we had it out and came out the other side better, but this ain't up for debate. He has intel we need, we can't get it here, so he's coming with. You drive. If you can handle a real truck that is." Sarge gets in the back, forcing Ian to put his head down.

Mark and Manny get in and start out the driveway that's more like its own road. Mark drives a few hundred yards when Sarge tells him to beep the horn four times. This letting Angel know to meet, and everything is ok. Code four he says. Ten miles away from the house at a Y in the road, they come to a stop at Sarge's request. A few moments later, the white SUV pulls up from the other side of the Y. Mark looks over to see Chris driving and Angel in the passenger seat. Seeing them brings a smile to his face.

 # What Now?

Still sitting on the road, Mark wants to know what's going on. He and Sarge get out telling Manny to stay in the car. Angel and Chris get out and they meet at the front of the two trucks.

"What is going on? Did I sleep through another planning meeting?" Mark scratches his head.

"So, the Ex here tipped me off that something wasn't right. When he walked past me, he swiped his hand across his neck in that old throat-cutting motion, telling me danger. I knew if he knew something, he'd fill Angel in, so I had to mark our path for them to follow." Sarge explains, getting a cigar out.

Chris starts to explain what he realized back at the cabin, "That guy had his shirt off when I walked in. I saw a tattoo and, growing up in Texas, knew it all too well. It was a Peckerwood tat. They are kinda a big thing down there, Aryan Brotherhood type group. I know if he was for real, he wasn't taking you guys anywhere good. So, I tipped Sarge off, got Angel and followed you..."

Angel stops him, "When we got close, you went inside. We saw the vehicle drive up but had no way to signal you... that is till you popped your head out the door." Angel smiles.

"Wait, you?" Mark points his finger at her.

"They had set up on you out there. I didn't know what was going on inside, so I didn't know who was friendly and who wasn't till I saw you and then them start shooting." Angel defends herself.

"You could have…" Mark stops himself, "I guess it is you, and if I trust anyone to shoot at my head it would be you." He smiles at her.

"Near your head…" She corrects him.

Turning their focus back to what to do next, "What now?" Mark asks.

"We go back. There are too many supplies there to leave. Enough food for our group for months and enough ammo to keep us in the fight long term. If we don't go back, they will, and we can't let them be better supplied and possibly out number us." Sarge says heading to his truck.

Manny unable to follow the order walks up, "But we just had at least a hundred Zeeks surround us. We want to go back to that?" Manny reverts to his old doubtful self.

"Manny, he's right. If we can hole up at the cabins and not need to go look for food, we can keep the kids and all of us safe. You saw how much ammo and gear was in there. We'd be set for a long while and something tells me we'll need it." Mark says reassuringly.

Chris, Manny, and Angel jump in the truck with Sarge while Mark follows alone in his SUV. His feeling of being watched has him on edge. As they retrace the path they blazed out of the danger, Mark can't help but wonder how they got all the people down there. Did they go in alive or were they already dead? Is that why the town was so empty? Is that where they came from at the hotel? Who could do something like that? There had to be a lot of them to work that out. As they arrive at the edge of the property, the trucks come to a dusty stop. Chris pops out, standing on the sidestep of the tall truck. Using a set of binoculars, he scouts the risk ahead.

Both trucks begin to pull forward, Chris and Angel get out and walk out ten feet in front, scanning all areas. Just like before, the benefit of this place is how open it is for some distance. They'd be able to see something coming from a ways off. The lack of live bodies must have caused the pack of Zeeks to move on, all but a few slow movers have gone. They pull up to the barricade and park. Sarge climbs out "Mark, Angel, you two set security! Keep numb nuts in the car and don't let any Zeeks crawl up our asses!" Sarge yells.

Manny and Chris follow Sarge inside. They start to bring out the food first; box after box of canned goods and the meals ready-to-eat. The back of Mark's truck is nearly full and they have only made six or so trips. Sarge and Chris start on weapons and ammo, while Manny continues to haul out food. Ten minutes go by and the increased activity inside and noise outside have stirred up some of the Zeeks in the woods. Still a good distance off, Angel tells the boys to hurry up.

Loaded up with as much as they can carry, it's time to get out of here. Angel gets in with Mark, and Chris and Manny ride with Sarge, much to the dislike of Manny. They pull away, Mark looks in the mirror at the house, imagining how a nice family had lived there. Kids out front chasing a dog around. A mom standing on the front porch with a pitcher of sweet tea. A dad rolling around the back of the house on his tractor, and everyone piling on as he puts it in gear and it hops and bounces out into the field, the dog now chasing after them. However, now its bullet hole and paint chip ridden and surrounded by burnt dead bodies and scorched ground. He thinks to himself, *how did we get here and what do we have to do? Is this all that comes after? Death and fire and loss? This can't be all that's left...*

The ride back is somber in both trucks. In Mark's, it's a relationship that puts strain on everyone involved, but still feels good in these times of darkness. In Sarge's, no doubt, the thought of what's to come with their unwelcomed guest. They reach the turn off for the cabins, Sarge stops and gets out grabbing a bag out of the back of the truck, he then walks up to Mark who rolls the window down.

"Hey, I got some explosives from that house. Going to place some trip wire around here to keep this way safe, so get that asshole out of my truck and into the worst cabin up there; I'll be along shortly. Angel, you get in your perch. I want you on overwatch at least till it gets dark, then I want you back to camp. If we get in a fire fight, I don't want you on the wrong side of our fire." Sarge steps away from the SUV and waves his index finger in a circle, telling them to go.

Finally home after what was a way longer day than anyone had plans for, the group is happy to see the cabins. Chris gets out and starts to get Ian out. Mark points at the last cabin in the row, this one is long since inhabited. Even before all of this started, visitors would tell chilling campfire stories about it.

Manny goes to Elsa, "Hey, how are the kids?" He kisses her such love in this embrace.

"Good. You look dirty. What happened, and who is that guy?" She looks long and hard at him with fear in her eyes.

"Nothing. We ran into some trouble, but nothing we couldn't handle." He smiles.

"I hate you going out there, the angry one doesn't trust you or us. Mark is sweet, but he can't protect you. We need you to come home to us... we need you to stay home with us not out there where things want to eat you." She starts to tear up.

Looking at the brutalized man getting escorted into the decrepit cabin.

Manny and Elsa's daughter Grace runs up and gives Manny a big hug, "Daddy, you're back!" She yells.

"Yes, *mi hija*, I'm home. Did you do anything fun today?" Manny drops to one knee to look at Grace.

"Ryan showed me how to find poison ivy and what plants you can eat!" She says, overjoyed.

"Wow, that's cool! Glad you're making friends *mi hija*. Let's go inside and hang out for a bit while the other guys talk to our new guest." Manny stands and takes Elsa and Grace by the hand into their cabin. He knows what could happen next and doesn't want them, or himself, to be a part of it.

Mark watched that encounter then turned to look for his kids. Evelyn is close behind Chris escorting Ian into the cabin. Ryan hasn't appeared yet. Mark walks to his cabin and before he gets to the door Meg stops him.

"He's not in there... He walked off after we told him to stay close and to stop going off in the woods with Grace." Meg looks sad.

"The woods? Alone?" Mark looks around, worried.

"He loves going for walks. He knows this lake better than any of us, so if he doesn't want to be found he won't be..." She admits.

"How long has he been gone?" Panic sets in for Mark.

"Not long. Maybe five or ten minutes. He has been running off since you've been going out again. You didn't know that?" Meg looks at Mark, sadly.

"No. No one told me… and with everything going on I haven't really made time… I know where he is." Mark remembers he wanted to walk his favorite trail together.

Mark takes off running into the woods. Fear and regret fill his heart. As he runs down a trail that brought so much joy not so long ago, he dreads what he may find on it now. His footsteps clap off the ground like a horse at full gallop. Deeper into the woods than he'd hoped to go, and against his better judgment, Mark starts to call for Ryan. He slows as he comes to an opening in the trail. "Ry, I know you're out here. Remember you wanted to go for a walk together? Well now I'm here, so let's walk. Show me all the amazing things you know!" He calls out. After taking a few more steps he hears movement to his left, making a quick circle, Mark zeros in on the sound.

"Ry, look I know you haven't gotten to have as much fun as we'd both like you to have but it's dangerous out here for you. So please come out so we can get back, it's getting dark out here and then it will be very dangerous." Mark takes a few more steps towards the sound. "Ry?" Mark comes to a large downed tree trunk as he looks over it, GRRRRAWWWR! Mark falls back to the ground.

Coming over the top of the trunk at him an aged slower and more decayed Zeek reaches for him. Sliding back away from it on his butt kicking his feet, fear overwhelming him. AAWWWHHH! AARRRRWW! Getting closer Mark notices a small Pocket knife stuck in the Zeek's face, he recognizes it as the one Ryan was given. Just as all the worrisome thoughts leave Mark's mind the Zeek is on top of him… CHOOOOMP CHOOOMP! CLLLACK CLLLACK! The sound of teeth in his face. A gel like goo drips on his face.

Inside the chaos Mark hears, "Dad? DAD!" Ryan appears from inside the tree trunk. "Help! HELLLLP! he yells. Unsure of what to do he looks on as Mark tries to fight off this attack.

"Ry-an run, don't st-op till yo-u see yo-ur sist-er." Mark grunts out. "GO! NOW!" He yells using all his strength.

Ryan takes off feet moving as fast as they can, he yells for help the entire way, his voice fades in the distance.

Still in the grips of the fight, he rolls to the top position, the Zeek is strong and almost pushes him off just trying to reach him with his mouth. RAAWR OOOWWRRE RAAWR! Comes from behind Mark another one stumbles out of the woods. Ryan's yelling and the commotion from the fight must have stirred up the ones nearby. Another two fumble their way into the clearing.

One has Mark around the neck pulling him backwards, he looks over his shoulder and sees a woman's face, but the lower half looks as though it's been eaten, down to the bone in parts. Before he is pulled off the first Zeek he grabs the knife out of its cheek. Now armed he lets himself fall back and uses the fall to aid it sinking the knife into the woman's brain, she goes limp and he uncoils her arm from his neck.

"Ok you freaks, now it's a fight." Mark almost seems to enjoy himself. The two standing Zeeks look of equal age to the others. One, a male, is missing a hand and Mark takes notice to the hand it does have and sees a pair of hand cuffs. The other, another woman, doesn't look like she's been out in the

elements long. Her clothing looks clean apart from the normal Zeek goo. Mark rushes the handless one first shoving it out of arms reach. Swinging wildly the woman comes at him her eyes hooked on her next meal. Her face is unblemished apart from the look of being sickly, eyes sunk in, skin loose in some areas. Mark goes to grab her by the neck and drives the small knife down from the twelve o'clock position into her skull, THUNK! Her eyes go blank and mouth stops moving. As she falls Mark grips the knife tighter, but it still doesn't slide out as he'd needed it to.

Now with more urgency Mark yanks on the knife harder to dislodge it from the skull. SNAP! The handle brakes off. The Handless Zeek grabs Mark, opens his mouth wide to sink his teeth into Mark's neck. Mark closes his eyes. URRRR! The Zeek rears back, SPLAT. BANG! From off in the distance. Mark is covered in brain and blood.

"CLEAR!" A voice calls from the distance. Angel's voice, "Hey, you ok? Did you get bit?" She calls franticly.

Mark in disbelief responds, "No you saved me. It didn't get me. Ryan..."

"He's ok, he won't leave Ev's side now. I think this all just became real to him." She smiles at him.

"Thank you. I thought I was done for." Mark looks around at the bodies.

"Where did they come from? I haven't seen anything out this way, maybe one at a time. I haven't seen groups since back at the beginning." Angel investigates her kill.

Mark joins her, "Not sure I came across this one, and then these came out of nowhere." Mark points to the tree trunk.

"This one looks like it could have broken free from something or somewhere." She points at the blood on the handcuffs. "But these look like they've been inside for a long time. No rips on their clothing, no scrapes or cuts. Angel squats down and investigates a little more.

Mark sees a surprised look on her face, "What do you see?" He asks, also kneeling.

"Injection sites." She responds alarmed, "If I didn't know any better, I'd think these were being experimented on." She leans away cocking her head slightly.

"Let's go get Sarge and show him. See what he thinks in that uber paranoid brain of his." He stands and reaches his hand down to help Angel up.

Back at the Camp they look for Sarge. Before they get far Ryan runs up and hugs them both. Ryan takes a step back looking up at them with a smile, "Thank you, Miss Angel, for saving my dad. I knew you would."

"You're welcome little man, you did good coming to get me." Angel leans down to Ryan with a smile, "Did you stab that Zeek in the face?"

He whispers back to her, "Yes I know to go for the head…"

She smiles even bigger, "Next time go for the ear. It's a bigger target and its further from the mouth. We don't need you getting bit now do we." She pretends to bite him.

His giggle is reminiscent to Mark of when Rachel did just that to Ryan. Before he can think himself out of the happy feeling Evelyn hugs him from behind. She pulls him in closer her face rests on his back with a smile she says, "I guess there are worse things than you two being together. When Ryan came back screaming, I feared the worst. If you die, what then? I think you shouldn't feel bad if you have feelings for her dad. I know mom was… is the love of your life and part of me is a little mad at you but we don't live in that world anymore. This isn't stepmom or two Christmases. Mom is gone and you aren't, but you could be. If she gives you something else to fight for or if she fights for you harder, we have the best chance at having you home every night and that's something I am ok with."

Mark has a tear rolling down his cheek, "When did you become so smart?" Mark wipes the tear off his face.

"I've always been smart but didn't feel like I mattered enough to show it." Evelyn says.

Mark breaks the grip of the hug turns to look at Evelyn face to face, "Girl, you always matter. I never knew what you wanted. I never knew what Ry needed. I felt like I was just floating hoping your mom would pull through because she had all the answers. I was just along for the ride."

"Dad, mom may have been that for you but for us we needed you both." Evelyn realizes she's kept Mark from whatever it was he was on his way to do and looks over to Ryan. "Who were you looking for?"

"Oh! We need to find Sarge!" Mark Calls out to Angel, "Hey we need to get back out there before it gets too dark to track." Mark and Angel head to Sarge's cabin.

The trio of Mark, Angel, and Sarge head off into the woods. They take caution as they walk, guns at the ready. Sarge and Angel move like ghosts over the fallen leaves, Mark moves like a clumsy squirrel. The light is diming even with the bare trees. The smell reminds Mark of walking with his family around Thanksgiving, dreaming of a big dinner and football in the front yard.

November 30th, 2012

   Mark and Ryan are playing catch in the yard, for his age Ryan is good at catching and throwing the football. Ryan lets the ball fly in a perfect spiral right into Marks hands. Mark on the other hand isn't as good, his throws wobble and go either too high or too short.

   "Dad come on, I'm not that tall." Ryan turns to chase down the ball again. His next throw is another perfect one right to Mark's hands. "Hey dad, can I ask you something?"

   Mark manages to get the ball back to Ryan, "Yeah son, anything."

   Ryan holds the ball and looks at the ground, "So when you like a girl, how do you talk to her?" Ryan falls into a pool of embarrassment releasing a deep breath, "Every time I try to talk to her, I can't find my words and then I just feel dumb." When Ryan looks up Mark is walking to him.

   Laughing Mark puts his hand on the ball, "Hey son, I'm going to let you in on something. Boys never know what to say to girls, old ones, young ones, smart ones, and me, the dumb ones." Mark takes the ball from Ryan's hands, looks down at him smiling, "Let's go for a walk."

   The two go off to the alley path behind their house. Laughing and taking in the moment together, they talk about girls, they talk about cars, they even talk about life. Ryan has always been smart for his age and because of that has a hard time relating to kids his age. Most times he'd rather be alone, so he doesn't feel weird or awkward. He isn't an outcast at school, but kids don't go out of their way to be around him. That can be hard on a kid especially at the age of ten, when you start to develop into the preteen you're going to be.

"So, Ryan let me ask more about this girl." Mark slows the pace down a look of encouragement on his face. "What's her name?"

Ryan looks up all aglow, "Bri!" He smiles you can practically see the hearts circling his head.

"Tell me about her. What is it you like about her?" His voice is soft and inviting.

"Oh, man she's the prettiest girl in school. She has short hair. I think I heard her say it's a pixie stick cut. When we see each other at lunch, I think she smiles at me, but I'm not sure, you know? She has braces and they are red and yellow, my two favorite colors. Oh, and blue eyes. It makes me think of a vampire in a movie, I think that's cool."

"I think it's just called a Pixie cut, buddy. So, if you like her just tell her, but be respectful. She'll either like you back or she won't, and that's ok. If she doesn't like you, be nice and give her space." Mark speaking sincerely.

"Dad, I'm scared she doesn't like me and just thinks I'm weird." His eyes turn to the ground again.

They walk in silence, the birds that are still around chirping, wind pushing the leaves around the ground, the smell of fireplaces and burning leaves in the air. Mark, thinking of the right words to say, takes a few more steps then stops. "Son, in life things are going to be scary. If it doesn't scare you, it isn't important, and when it comes to girls you can't fight what you feel. You have one shot at life and if you want to, you make it one to remember. These are the chances you take. Don't let fear, or people, say you can't do something. Life will pass you by if you let that happen." Mark turns back towards the way they came. "Now, let's go get some dinner. What do you think mom made for us?"

Mark's ears begin to ring, Ryan's mouth is moving but it isn't his voice, "They're gone."

Mark seems confused, "No, Ryan they're at home. Mom is home with your sister." Mark squints as the woods change from a nice well-kept path to a clearing.

"No, Mark, those Zeeks are gone." The voice again comes out of Ryan's mouth. "Mark!"

Mark shakes his head, and that nice November evening is long gone.

Looking around he sees the tree trunk and looks over the area where the Zeeks should be but there is nothing, none on the ground. Sarge believes them, knowing and trusting in Angel.

"Break it down for me what happened." Sarge gets the report again.

"I don't understand, they should be right here." Mark kneels where the blood spray was when Angel saved him. "But nothing." Mark looks to Angel fear in his eyes, and for the first time in a long time hers as well.

"Sarge, they were here." Angel speaks with certainty in her voice and on her face.

Sarge looks at the ground almost like he's reading a map. "Look. We got at least a two-man team, moved the bodies. Went west out of this thicket. We don't have time to track them, they did a good job being light-footed on their way in, but the bodies made it harder to do on the way out."

"Dexter's people?" Mark looks around scanning the tree-line.

"Not sure. These men were well trained and organized." Sarge also scans the surrounding area.

They begin the trek back to the cabins. Sarge starts to fall to the back of the line, turning and walking backwards every ten steps, Mark is in front as they near the halfway point back. "Angel, take point!" Sarge yells. "Gun at the ready." Sarge ratchets up the intensity.

Angel doesn't hesitate on the order. Mark, now between the two isn't sure what to do so he stays quiet and steps as soft as he can. Sarge still walking backwards, head on a swivel clicks, the safety on his rifle from semi to full auto. Angel is also unsure of the threat she looks back at Sarge, then Mark. She cuts her look back to Sarge. He barks "Eyes front! Pick it up!"

They begin to run, arriving at the camp's edge. Sarge stops and sweeps left to right looking down the sights, ready to fire if need be. "Main cabin everyone. Now!" He calls out eyes still peering into the dark woods.

Understanding the seriousness of the situation, no one says a word as they all head inside. Sarge slowly makes his way in as well. Before he closes the door, he takes one more, quick glance around.

Sarge seems shaken like no one has ever seen, "Here's the deal, we have people out there. Not sure how many but sure as shit they're out there. I don't think its Dexter's backwoods, cousin-loving, dirt bag friends. These boys are good, they moved those bodies and waited for us to come back. They want something I'm not sure what, but they aren't leaving till they get it." Sarge puts on a brave face.

Chris looks concerned, "Don't get me wrong I would follow you into hell Sarge, but what's got you so spooked?"

"Son, I'm not going to lie these boys got behind me on the way back. Didn't hear them, see them, nothing." Sarge for the first time drops his head in shame.

Mark seeing Sarge's dejections chimes in, "Look man you are the best of the best. We've been going 100 miles per hour all day. Just tell us what to do next" Mark stands tall.

Sarge looks to Angel, knowing what he has to do but every fiber in his body tells him not to because she's his blood and he loves her, "I don't want to send you, but we need overwatch out there. Stay close and alert." Sarge instructs with tenderness in his voice.

She responds, "On it, Sir." She smiles a forgiving smile and grabs her rifle.

"Radio silence, two clicks all clear, one click, contact. Be safe out there, girl.

Angel steps to the door Mark tries to stop her, but she keeps moving. He watches the door close and looks back at Sarge. "She's locked in now, don't take it personal Mark." Sarge has a new-found conviction in his voice.

Meg hugs Sarge, she's wrapped around his midsection and he has one arm pulling her in. Meg looks up at him to ask, "She's going out there alone?"

"That's what she does…" Sarge smiles with pride, "That's who she is, and I love her."

Mark walks toward Sarge and Meg, his footsteps loud on the old cabin floor, "You have to be kidding me? We could be surrounded by who knows how many people and you're going to just send her out alone?" Mark now looking Sarge in his eyes.

Sarge removing his arm from Meg, puffing his chest as he does so, "Mark, we've done this before, you ended up on the ground out cold. Now she's got her orders and that's that. You want to help her, don't give her a reason to question her orders. She's a Marine Scout Sniper, some of the best to do it."

Mark knowing a fight isn't something he'll win starts to change his approach. His tone of voice is still strong, but body less combative, "Look they're sending Zeeks in here. We don't know how many are out there, shouldn't we do two-person watches or something?"

Sarge smiles and accepts the terms of Mark's surrender, "We have that bag of dicks in the other cabin to deal with. We have a choice."

Chris speaks up from the sofa, sitting between Evelyn and Ryan, "A choice about what?"

"I had questions for that guy, but things have changed. This isn't his crew no way. Dexter was smart and planed but they weren't trained like he was." Sarge scans the room avoiding eye contact.

Evelyn is the first to ask what he has in mind. His avoidance of answering is off-putting. Mark, also growing impatient of what's not being said, opens his mouth to speak, but before he can Chris answers for Sarge, "We kill him. We kill him, right?"

Chapter:6 # Is This Us Now?

"That's right. Kill Ian" Sarge says plainly.

The group is floored by the thought of this. No one says anything for what seems like hours. The fire in the fireplace is the only sound in the room, its hisses and crackles filling the strained silence. Ryan gets up to go to the bathroom, his head is hung. He feels the sadness in the room but doesn't quite understand why. His departure stirs up enough activity in the room to get everyone to snap back into the world.

"What we are talking about is out right murder." Meg looks at Sarge in disgust.

"I know what I'm saying, but if we have to worry about him and whoever's out there too… we will make a mistake." Sarge tries to reason with the thoughts in his own head as much as the rest of the room.

Sarge sits at the dining table in an old wooden chair. Mark is sitting across from him, neither one able to look at the other. Thoughts of Joey and Angel running through Marks mind bringing both sorrow and hope for what could be, cloud his views on the subject.

Meg, who has moved almost as far away from Sarge as safely possible sits in an old armchair close to the fireplace. She repeats herself, "Outright MURDER!"

Mark, unhappy with this conversation going on with Ryan within earshot, "Keep your voice down, Ryan doesn't need to hear this." Mark looks to the hallway that Ryan went down minutes ago.

Evelyn turns to the hallway as well, "Is he still in there? He's been gone a while, right?"

Chris puts his hand on her thigh and helps himself up, "I'll go check on him." Chris walks down the hall and knocks on the door, KNOCK. KNOCK. "Ry, you ok in there? Did you fall in or are you stuck in your zipper?" He receives no response. He starts to turn the doorknob, "Did you clog the toilet?" Chris jokes opening the door. To his surprise the bathroom is empty, and the window is open, he runs to the open window and looks out. He charges back into the living room, "He's gone! He went out the window!"

Mark gets up so fast he flips his chair over. "Where would he go?"

Everyone bursts out of the cabin running in all directions searching and looking into the dark night for the smallest member of their family. Manny and his family come out of their Cabin after hearing the noise, Meg tells them Ryan is missing. They also join the search. Mark starts down the Path where he found Ryan the last time a voice in the distance stops him, "Here, he's here." Its Sarge, he's standing on the steps of the cabin they continue to use as a jail cell. Mark runs, meeting up with the rest at the steps.

"What are you doing over here? It's dangerous you know that, right?" Mark grabs Ryan with aggression and hugs him.

Still on one knee Mark askes Sarge how he found him, "I thought about what I would do if I wanted to help. This kid was going to end the debate for us."

Mark, in shock looks at Ryan, "Is that true?"

"You guys are always fighting, and you always say we need to stick together. I was sitting there thinking about something you said to mom, then again to me once, 'sometimes I have to do things that scare me, to protect you. Sometimes I do the hard job, so you don't have to.' I just wanted everyone to be happy again. I'm sorry dad." Ryan looks at his shoes, pulling a small gun from his pants.

Mark grabs it and lifts Ryan's head up with one finger under his chin. Pulls him close, "It's ok son, it's all ok. I know you just want to help. The more I try and keep you a kid the harder you fight back. Your mom was always better at that. Come now its late and if you're going to be a man tomorrow, you'll need your sleep tonight." Mark leads him back to the cabin, "I'll be back Sarge."

Along the way Mark keeps Ryan close and in a loving embrace. Once in bed Mark goes to kiss Ryan on his forehead but stops, and reaches with his hand for a handshake, "Sorry, I forgot you're a man now."

"No, it's ok. It makes things feel like life is normal. It's bad enough Ev is nice to me all the time, I can't have you acting funny now too." Ryan rolls over then quickly turns back to his father, "Dad, I miss mom so much. I try to keep it in and not give you something else to worry about... but I really miss her. Her hugs, her jokes, but most of all the way she made me feel." Sniffles come from the boy who rolls to face away from Mark to not show the weakness. With a splintering heart Mark leaves the room taking one last look at the glow in the dark stars stuck to the ceiling and model airplanes and rockets hanging. He closes the door.

The long walk back to the group is hard and heavy on Mark. As he arrives, he looks at Sarge, anger and pain fill him. He pushes past everyone into the cabin, draws his weapon and, BANG!

One shot rings out. No words were spoken, no pleas of mercy granted. Mark walks out of the cabin, "There its done. I'm going to bed."

The group looks on as Mark walks away. Chris looks at Evelyn, "Is this who we are now?" She cries.

The sun is low in the sky, but Mark is awake. The feeling of eyes on him snatches him into the cold early morning. He rolls in the bed to see the doorway and a person standing in it, his eyes adjust to the predawn light. Angel is standing in the doorway. She looks to be shaking, and Mark is unsure what Angel he's seeing. Is it the one that jokes and had goals in life beyond killing at long distances, or the one that coldly leaves the room without a word or even a look of softness? None of this matter as she walks toward the bed, she pauses, like a vampire waiting for an invite into a home. The faint morning light hitting one side of her face. Mark can see she's been crying. He lets out a sigh and gets up on his knees and pulls her close, grips her tight, and hugs her as if there is no tomorrow. Her hands cold on Mark's body. She seems like her whole world has just come crashing down around her inside the circle of his embrace. Marks eyes had been closed during this hug when he opens them, he sees Rachel looking back at him in a photograph on the wall. He remembers his feelings and lets Angel go.

"What's wrong Angel." He quickly starts a dialog to distract from the awkward moment.

"I... You, you can't become this. I need you to be not this, not more of the same thing I've always known." She sits down on the edge of the bed.

Mark also swings his legs over the edge of the bed pulling the blankets to cover his legs, "What do you mean." Mark asks as if he doesn't remember killing a man in cold blood just hours ago.

"I heard what you did. I know it had to be done and I know you were angry, but that isn't you. It can't be, I don't want it to be." She sinks lower.

"Listen, Angel. What I did wasn't from anger, it was from sadness. Looking at Ryan convinced he had to kill someone, it broke me, and I just wanted to end it. I remember his blood on my hands and in my nose, the way it felt when it hit my face, warm and thick. It doesn't matter now because it's a new day, right?"

Angel gets up and looks at Mark in disbelief heart beginning to break for him, "You can't believe that. Can you?"

"You showed me last night that we have to do things, things that we know are wrong or dangerous, but we do them." Mark gets up and puts pants on.

Anger in her voice, "This is different, and you know it." Angel walks away from Mark.

Still bare chested, he follows her across the room standing just a few steps behind her "Why is it different? Because you were following an order?" Hints of sarcasm drip from his words.

"Yes, I was doing what I was told to keep you safe, your kids safe. What you did was cold, one step closer to evil. I've seen it happen on the battlefield. I can't watch it happen here." Angel turns to Mark looking up into his eyes.

Standing chest to chest now, "That's just it. I don't know who I am in the world, this world is dirty and now I am too. I lost my wife less than six months ago, and here I am... it's taking everything I have not to kiss you. I would have never thought about that before this world."

"You aren't dirty Mark. You are the cleanest thing in this world." Her gaze softens, "How can you not see that? Sarge,

Chris, the others, your kids, we all do whatever we can to keep you that way because you give us hope. Hope that we aren't all lost and bloody and sad for no reason. Mark, you shine in the dark." Angel looks around the room at all the pictures of Rachel, "You know the only reason I haven't kissed you is out of respect for these eyes looking at me everywhere I go. No offense, but Rachel seems like the type of woman to kill me in my sleep even from the grave."

Mark smiles, "You aren't wrong." Mark hugs Angel again.

After the hug she laces her fingers in with Mark's and pulls him toward the door. Nothing is settled, "Come, let's get some coffee and food, you know, I'd kill for some of those weird pancakes you made when we first got here."

With a laugh Mark replies, "Weird? They were whole wheat."

"Yeah, like I said, weird."

In the main room they find Chris and Evelyn sleeping on the sofa. Chris is the big spoon, his arm around Evelyn like a seat belt keeping her from falling off the edge. Ryan is still asleep in his bed. Mark tip toes to the coffee maker, the wood floor still creaks and moans. Angel opens the pantry and gets a can of coffee out, there are fifteen cans of coffee stacked on a shelf along with peanut butter, tubes of chips, cereal boxes, and other long shelf-life foods. Angel hands Mark the coffee, and he hands her the pot to get water.

She glides to the sink taking a moment to look out of the window to her right, it's a window that looks out of the front of the cabin overlooking the lake. A smile appears on her face, her eyes turn to the ground and then the sink.

Mark lost in her beauty, "What are you smiling at?" He walks up and puts his arms around her.

Turning around in his grip to drink in his sweetness, Angel says, "I never thought I'd be here."

"None of us thought we'd be living in a movie about the dead walking." Mark giggles.

"No dork. Here in this kind of a moment. Making morning coffee with a guy in a cabin on a lake." Her smile returns, "We never had this as kids. Dad would wake us up and we'd train, or he'd be going off to work and tell us the list of stuff that had to be done before he got home." Angel lays her head on Mark's chest. He wraps his arms around her tighter. K-THUNK.

A car door closing grabs their attention. They both walk to the window looking out. They see Sarge loading up gear in his truck. They waste no time heading out to ask what's going on. The cold morning sucks the warmth out of them. Sarge barely acknowledges them as he keeps loading the truck. He seems more off than normal.

Mark looks to Angel for guidance, to no avail, "Hey what's up?" Mark mutters.

Sarge doesn't slow down to reply, he just keeps marching on, heavy boot steps clunking on the damp dirt. Sarge waves to Meg to get in the truck. She has a bag too, much bigger of a bag than needed for a day mission.

"Marlin! Talk to me." Mark stands in Sarge's way.

Displeased in being called by his real name, "Look Mark, right now we are all off our axis. I can't find my pull back to true north. I think it's us, this. I don't know who or how to be in whatever this is." Sarge steps around Mark to close the tailgate.

A cold wind whips off the lake, but it's not near as cold as Sarge is being.

Mark turns to follow Sarge, seeing the pain in his eyes, "Let's talk about this, we can work this out."

As Sarge opens the driver's door he smirks, "We sound like women in a breakup, look you were right I shouldn't have sent Angel out there like that, but you were wrong in killing Ian. At least the way you did."

Mark angry at the last statement, "You said it needed to happen. I am trying to step up, isn't that what you wanted?"

Sarge growing even more angry, "You don't get it. Me sending Angel out had to happen, we needed eyes out there. You killing him like that isn't who you're supposed to be."

Mark getting the same speech from Sarge he got earlier becoming sick of being told who he should be, "And who am I supposed to be?"

Angel reminded of the last few times the two men got into an argument, steps up to the door as well, "Look you both did stuff you wish you hadn't, that's over, done. Now let's put it away and move on."

"That's what I'm doing. Moving on." Sarge goes to close the door, but Mark grabs it stopping it just before it does.

"Where the hell are you going to go?" Mark asks.

"That house is just sitting there. Better it goes to the good guys than the assholes who had it right? I took care of Ian's body for you." Sarge slams the door with authority. Looking down at Mark sadness visible on his face.

Mark and Angel stand back looking at Sarge confused. Sarge rolls the window down, "Look this isn't goodbye, think of it as if one camp gets attacked, we have backup on the way. All we have to do is hold the line and the cavalry is coming."

"We are stronger together." Mark says sadly.

Sarge looks at Meg then Angel, "Looks to me neither of us is alone Mark. Watch her six, you hear me?"

"Don't go, Dad" Angel says tears in her eyes.

"This ain't forever girl. I gotta do what I gotta do." Sarge rolls up the window locking up his emotion and pulls off, with a loud rumble of his truck getting further and further away, it feels real, the mood is heavy for both Angel and Mark.

The cabin door squeaks and Chris and Evelyn step onto the small porch, "Where's he going?" Chris calls out.

Mark fills them in, and they all retreat inside, feeling sad and worried. Once inside the smell of coffee fills the room, but the fear of what's next fills it more. Ryan pops in the room, "Why's everyone so sad?" He asks while getting cereal out of the pantry.

Ryan grabs a bowl and starts in on his food like it's just a normal day in a normal world, reading the comic on the back of the box giggling to himself. The others are stuck watching him, thinking, how does he just keep going as if the world isn't over and awful?

"Why are you all staring at me?" Ryan asks mouth full of dry cereal.

"Kid, I want to be like you when I grow up." Chris jokes.

"But you are grown up?" Ryan tilts his head, "Do we still have those juice boxes?" He starts back in on his food.

Mark starts to get up, Angel stops him "I got it." She smiles at Mark.

The day goes by like a flash. Before the group knows it, its dusk. This is the first day in what feels like weeks maybe months where something didn't go wrong or killing wasn't the pastime. They spent most of the chilly day playing board games and swapping stories. Manny and his family joined in part way into Chris telling a story about the time he had to run from the cops without pants on. After, he and the kids spent time playing with blocks in Ryan's room.

Mark got a fire going in the fireplace, Elsa made a rice dish that tasted like tacos. Laughter and joy now take the place of the sadness that had filled this very room just hours before.

Sitting around the dining room table like it's a holiday or a big family dinner, the group talking, joking and forgetting the world outside. Mark, leaning into Angel's ear says, "Maybe he was right. I think we all feel less anxious."

With mixed feelings she replies, "I'm still worried about them though. Aren't you?" Angel puts her hand in Mark's.

The volume in the room masks their voices, "Of course, but you have to admit, we had a nice quiet day today. I know you enjoyed it." Mark bumps her leg with his.

Angel, unable to hide her smile, "Yes, I did. It was nice to feel normal. But it can't last. Those people are still out there somewhere, and whoever is playing games with the Zeeks is too."

"There it is. The Angel we all know." Mark says jokingly.

"Oh, shut up. You know you've been thinking it too." Angel looks around the table at everyone happy for the first time in so long.

"Hey, you want to stay over tonight?" Mark quickly changes the subject.

"You sure?" Angel is shocked but also excited. Fear and a happy nervous energy wash over her.

Mark laughs, "It's not a wedding ring. It's you sleeping next to me sleeping."

"Yes, I'd like that." Angel smiles big, so big it grabs the attention of everyone else.

"And what is going on over there?" Elsa askes.

Evelyn responds for the blushing couple, "I think they finally took a first step."

The awkward pause leaves everyone playing with the remaining food on their plates. Manny, not one for such moments, gets up and offers to take people's plates off the table. Chris gets up next, he decides to take the first night watch picking up his shotgun and starting for the door.

Mark stops him offering a new idea. "You all slept here last night, what if we just all stay in this cabin and no one has to be out in the cold? Someone can keep watch from inside." Chris takes him up on the offer and no one else disagrees.

The group gets sleeping arrangements, Manny and his family will be in Evelyn's room, the kids in Ryan's and Evelyn and Chris in the main room. Mark and Angel had already come to an agreement of their own.

The kids go down first, fighting sleep but losing. Next, Manny falls asleep in the armchair by the fire. Elsa, Chris, Evelyn, Angel, and Mark continue the conversation. Elsa tells them stories about Manny that he'd object to if he was awake. After she feels she's had her fun she walks Manny to bed. Mark and Angel have put off this first date feeling long enough, and head to bed as well.

Their door closes and their world gets smaller, so small in fact it only has room for two people. Mark and Angel look at each other fully clothed and neither one is ready to make that first move to undress. Mark giggles, "This morning you came in here and I was already in my boxers but now I feel like I can't even take my shirt off." He does just that like he's done testing the water at a pool and just jumps in.

Angel is still hesitant, so Mark turns around. She accepts his chivalrous act. As his back is turned, he can see her reflection in the picture frame on the wall. He realizes it was a photo of Rachel he had taken. His eyes go to the ground. The bed becomes noisy as Angel climbs in, her clothes in a pile at the foot of the bed. Mark turns to look at her. The feeling of a schoolboy being around his crush for the first-time washes over him. He takes a few steps toward the bed, stopping and asking, "Do you snore?" Uncontrollable laughter fills the room as he climbs into bed. Her cool to the touch body is a balance to his warm almost hot feeling. Fire and water coming together to make steam. She falls asleep faster than any night in recent memory. Mark on the other hand, Mark can't help but look at the beauty lying beside him. Capable of such violence, such cold almost robotic emotion. Somehow, he is still drawn into the look of peace on her face. No anger, no sadness, no anything. Just Angel in her rawest form.

Thinking to himself, *Rachel would like you, hell she may have even joked about leaving me for you. I still can't shake the feeling that this is wrong. My heart wants this, but my head tells me this is too soon. I could die tomorrow and that'd be it. She could die, and from the way she talks, never having been told 'I love you' by someone not just saying it out of obligation. I'm just worried I'm too normal for you. Ha, the dead walk and I'm laying here awake because of a girl.*

His mind drifts to thoughts of Joey, thoughts that turn into nightmares.

The almost forgotten sound of birds singing, wakes Mark. His eyes fall open on Angel still sleeping. Angel is normally first up and last down. Her being still asleep is an amazing thing. As Mark's senses turn on one by one, the morning is cold, an overcast sky makes it dim in the room. Resisting the want to stay in bed, Mark knows there are jobs to do and people to take care of.

Mark takes a deep breath and rolls out of bed, the second his feet hit the floor a feeling of dread overwhelms him. Still he stands shaking it off. The cool floor moans under his weight. The cabin is extremely silent, and a chill fills it. Mark starts to pull his clothes out of the old wood dresser, as he opens the drawer it creaks. He turns to see if it woke the sleeping Angel. Her eyes are still closed but she rolls a bit pulling the covers up closer to her face.

Mark goes back to getting dressed. After pulling his shirt down he heads for the door almost floating across the floor. His hand touches the doorknob and looks behind him one last time. Before he can turn his head, he feels arms slide under his and two hands on his chest. The angel of death with her stealth turned to ten, pulls him in with a strong grip.

"You're almost as quiet as me, when I was a kid." Angel smiles as she rests her head on his back.

Mark breaks her grip and turns to face her. He wraps his arms around her, her still warm from under the covers skin meets his now cold touch. Her body reacts to this in a shiver.

"Cold, your hands are freezing." Angel yelps.

"Yeah, fall is almost over I think." Mark replies. His hands slide down the small of her back, coming to rest on her hips.

"Mark last night was nice. I don't think I've slept that nice in months." Angel steps to her clothes on the floor at the foot of the bed, her bare chest reactive to the cold with goosebumps. Her body is fit, the faint outline of abs and the definition in her arms is like a magnet attracting Marks gaze. She turns and bends over at her waist, her back is muscular. Marks eyes go to her butt covered in white boy shorts. She looks over her shoulder, "Mark, are you checking out my ass?"

"Umm, no I was just looking at the, umm." He stumbles over his words, "I'm going to make coffee, do you want some?" He heads to the door again.

Now in the kitchen getting coffee ready, Mark looks out the window at the leafless tree limbs blowing in the breeze. The whistle of the wind echoing down the chimney. Angel walks out of the hallway, asking if she should start a fire, while Mark cooks. Mark smiles at this caveman era role reversal. The noise wakes everyone in the main room, the cold strikes everyone the same and they have no problem being woken up by Angel starting a fire.

Manny, feeling more a part of the group with Sarge out of the picture walks in and offers to do a perimeter sweep. Chris offers up his shotgun and Mark hands him a cup of coffee. With a smile Manny opens the door, the words I love you roll off his lips to Elsa. Before she can respond... Blood and hot coffee fill the air. TWWA! Manny's body hits the ground after a single shot rings out.

"On the ground, NOW!" Angel yells

Mark crawls towards the door as Chris crawls to Manny, who is writhing in pain on the floor. Chris grabs Manny by his belt and pulls him from the doorway. Mark kicks the door shut; the coffee cup goes flying off the porch.

 "He was on the ground before I heard the shot, where's he hit?" Angel says from the other side of the room. She's stuck on the far side because of the window. She could chance moving but doesn't want to be seen.

 Chris is applying pressure to the wound, "Right shoulder, no exit. Bullet is still in there. I think it missed the important stuff." Chris rips part of his shirt to help slow the bleeding.

 Hysterical, Elsa is crying. Evelyn is holding her back from getting up. The kids startled awake walk out of the hall. Mark gets up and runs to them, "Get down!" He jumps on them. Glass sprays into the room as the window explodes into from another shot.

 Angel rolls to her belly and crawls to the window looking out quickly. She reaches up and pulls the curtains closed. Evelyn lets go of Elsa.

 Elsa runs to Manny. Chris tells her to keep pressure to the gunshot, he goes to the kitchen for a knife. Angel looks to Mark who is still ushering the kids back in the hall.

 "Look guys this is going to get a whole lot worse before it gets better. She peeks out the window as the wind blows the curtains.

"What do you see?" Evelyn asks.

 "Looks to be 10 maybe 15 Zeeks moving in. Can't tell where the shot came from but they're a ways off." Angel scans the room with her eyes.

 Chris grabs a small paring knife, "Mark give me a hand getting him to the back room. I need to try and get the bullet out and stop the bleeding." Chris moves quickly.

"I'll get the first aid kit from the bathroom." Ryan pops out of the hall.

"Thanks kid. Ev, you start the stove and see if you can find some pliers and a needle and thread." Chris says picking Manny up by his legs as Mark grabs him by the torso.

Manny grunting in agony, "I love you girls, I love you. I love you." He keeps repeating.

Elsa is frozen at the edge of the hall as they take Manny back. Angel yells at her, "Hey, grab a gun. ELSA! Grab a gun! I need you."

Elsa looks around confused, "Me? I've never shot a gun before..."

Angel rolls her eyes, "Look, do you want him to die?"

"No!" Elsa responds with fire.

"If we don't keep the Zeeks back he's dead anyway. I need your help. Can you patch up a bullet hole?"

Elsa looks lost, "No?"

"Chris can. Are you strong enough to hold Manny down while Chris digs that bullet out?"

"No!" Elsa becoming more agitated.

"Mark can. Evelyn knows where things are in this cabin, you don't, so all I have is you. Here." Angel hands her one of the hunting rifles, it's a wood stock semiautomatic rifle.

Elsa looks at it like it will fall apart or go off in her hand, "Look this is the safety, this is the trigger. Point the angry end at what you want dead and pull the trigger. Most important don't shoot me. Now go to Ryan's room and be ready to shoot out that window when I say so. Stay LOW." Angel looks out the window one more time. "Go, now."

Evelyn walks past Elsa going the other way, she cuts a "Oh boy" look at Angel. She continues her search for the items Chris needs. Angel grabs the M4 that Mark normally carries and pokes the barrel out the window. Evelyn leaves the room.

Chris and Mark are now in the back room. This room is more of a nook than a room. It has just enough space for a cot and small table. Manny is in and out of consciousness on the cot. Chris directs Mark to hold Manny's shoulder down. Ryan hands Chris the first aid kit. First thing Chris does is grab a bottle of alcohol and pour some on the knife and pliers, as well as his hands. He then pulls the bloody shirt scrap off the wound. Chris starts to cut away Manny's shirt.

Now Chris has a better look at the wound. He wipes away the blood, and before he can pull the rag away blood pools in the area again. "Mark, I need you to put pressure on his brachial artery. I need to slow the bleeding enough to get a look at the damage. Put your hand around under his upper arm and with your fingers grab firm." Mark follows the instructions; Chris wipes the blood away again this time the wound stays clear.

"Ok, keep your hand there and hold him down with the other. Sorry brother, but this is going to be unpleasant..." Chris reaches in with his finger to see if he can find the bullet. Manny springs up and howls in agony, finally passing out from the pain. Chris has a "reaching into a couch for change" look on his face, tongue poking out and looking up. He asks Evelyn to go heat up the knife. After locating the bullet, he pulls his finger out. It didn't hit anything, and it isn't too deep either. Evelyn returns with the knife.

"Ok, here we go..." Chris pours some of the alcohol into the gunshot, then uses the pliers to reach in and grab the bullet.

"NOW!" they hear Angel yell. The sound of scattered gun fire fills the cabin.

"Ev, go see if they need anything." Mark says. "Chris and I got this."

Chris pulls the pliers out, "Got it!"

"Nice. Now what?" Mark asks.

"Now I stop the bleeding and close'er up." He does just that, using the hot knife to cauterize the wound.

The gunfire stops and the two men feel some hope. Chris starts to stitch the wound, "Mark get some of that gauze and tape out so we can bandage this up quick." Chris snaps the tail of the thread with his fingers. Pours a little more alcohol on the closed wound and places the bandage on it. "We'll need to keep an eye on him for a while, but I think he should be ok. We're looking for fever, milky discharge, smell, that kinda stuff. Let's go see what's going on out there. Ryan stay with Manny I trust you to keep him safe." Ryan jumps at the responsibility.

Mark and Chris head out in the main room, "Bout time!" Angel jokes. "We got Maybe 25 out there now. No way they found us by chance. Someone brought them here."

"Yeah, I got one guess who..." Mark fills with anger

"Good news, bad news. Good news, we're all together." Angel smirks.

"And the bad news?" Chris asks picking up his shotgun off the ground where it landed.

"We're trapped without knowing where the shooter is. It's not safe to move, too many Zeeks to run anyway. The way I see it we need to hold the position till the big guns get here." Angel says looking at Mark.

"Big guns? Sarge?" Mark smiles. "Oh boy, we'll never hear the end of this…"

"I know, but that's the only way out. Manny can't move and we have kids." A softer side of the warrioress shows.

"Copy that." Chris speaks up.

Mark looks around for his gun, "Is that mine?" He looks at Angel.

"Yeah, bout time I got my hands on your gun." She says smugly.

Evelyn shakes her head, "I'm going to go sit with Elsa she is probably losing it in there." She rolls her eyes and leaves the uneasy room.

Chris, Angel and Mark remain in the main room, fifteen minutes pass after the shooting stopped. They have tried to keep silent, the now disinterested army outside their walls has replenished their forces. Mark looked out last and his count was thirty-five Zeeks wandering about the lake-front cabin development. They bump into the table, SUV, and various other stationary things. Growls, moans, and groans are the playlist that is stuck on repeat for the group.

Angel has grown bored of the waiting game and watching Mark and Chris attempt to play paper football from an unrealistic distance away from each other. She whispers, "I'm going to go make sure the girls aren't sleeping in there." She starts to walk softly.

Chris pegs her with the paper football in the back of the head, "Hey, have Elsa go sit with Manny now. I'm sure Ryan is over it back there."

With not so nice eyes Angel nods her head. Within seconds Ryan pops around the wall separating the room from the hall.

He has the rifle Elsa had. Mark's face ruffles, eyes enlarge. Ryan knowing what the look means hands the rifle to Chris in disappointment.

 "Kid, you'll get to shoot soon enough." Chris says as he tucks the rifle under his arm.

 Mark pulls Ryan in for a hug, "It's not that I don't trust you, it's that I want you as far away from the fighting as you can be." Mark speaks softly.

 "But Dad..." A sad kid voice fights through the hug.

 "Mark, it might not be a bad idea to teach him how to use it. I mean that kinda stuff was normal when I was his age and we didn't have dead critters trying to eat us back then." Chris says country accent thick.

 "Why is it that I never have back up anymore?" Mark gives into the good argument. Ryan excitedly runs over to Chris.

 Mark watches as Chris and Ryan bond over the old hunting rifle. The look of joy on Ryan's face changes Mark's expression from apprehension to wonderment. Thinking to himself; *I was never a gun person. Not that I hated them just never had a use or want personally for them. I have to say it is fun to shoot when my life isn't depending on it. I guess there are worse things Ryan could be asking to learn about.* Mark watches until the midmorning light brightens the room almost as much as the smiles on both Chris and Ryan's faces. Mark, wanting to check on Evelyn and Angel pops around the hall corner, stopping just outside the door. This part of the hall is dark and narrow. He can see Elsa and Grace sitting at Manny's bedside, the small clip-on desk light sets them a-glow. The soft warm light makes them look like a play or one of those tiny scenes people put up at Christmas. He smiles, then remembers why he was standing there. Looking into the room Evelyn and Angel are in he sees

Ryan's bed pushed to the side, it was almost under the window. The room is a bit more lit because only blinds cover the window. He can see Evelyn but not Angel. Before he turns to walk away, he hears the mumbles of a low spoken conversation.

"So look Ev, I know we didn't exactly get off to a good start. I just want you to know how much I regret that. I see the steps you take to try and get along with me, and trust me I know that's not easy, believe me, I know."

Evelyn shifts, "It isn't that I don't like you, or don't want you and my dad to be… whatever you are. Being here, seeing all the things that my mom picked out, or remembering the two of them together here, before she got sick and it was always just fun, it's hard to see."

"I get that. One time when my dad brought a woman home. me and my brother, we said we'd set the table. Sarge, being him knew we were up to something. We super glued her fork and knife but not her spoon to the table." Angel laughs, probably louder than she should have, then continues, "So here we are, me, my brother, this rando lady, and Sarge. So, she goes for the knife first. It doesn't move, next the fork, same thing." More giggles, Angel almost in tears telling the story. Evelyn into the story as well as Mark just outside the room in the dark hallway, "So she laughs, 'haha guys very funny.' She says. She goes for the spoon saying 'pick on your dad's lady friend and…' she, I shit you not, full force tries for the spoon and knocks herself backwards out of her chair. Bloody nose, food everywhere. Sarge was pissed!"

Evelyn smiles, "I didn't know you had a brother."

"I just told you we parent trapped my dad's girlfriend and that's what you took from the story?" Angel wipes tears of laughter from her gray eyes.

"I guess. Mostly I realized I didn't really know much about you beyond what I've seen." Evelyn plays with her foot in the well-worn and dingy carpet.

"The moral of the story is, I've done worse, am worse than you. So, don't feel like you don't have the right to feel how you feel. Your mom died, mine straight up left because she didn't love us. We still didn't want to see our dad with someone else." Angel looks Evelyn in her eyes not knowing they are Rachel's as well.

"Can I ask you something?" Evelyn now moving closer to Angel.

Angel moves closer in kind, "Sure, anything."

"Why? Why my dad?"

Angel smiles and looks at the ground, her grey pants and black boots swish and clunk as she repositions herself, "In my life, my entire life only one person didn't make me feel like a piece of crap. I'm a bitch, I don't like people much, I was never the girl that fit in... boys wanted to have sex with me but didn't care to know me past my body. Until..." Evelyn smiles and stops her.

"Till, my dad." She looks over at Angel.

"Yeah, he looks past all that crap, hell he fought my dad, and still wants to be with me, I think. He makes me feel like all those movies describe." Angel lights up and blushes a bit.

"My mom said the same thing, that's who he is. He doesn't care about just part of something. He loves all of it. But he is still broken. He may never be fixed again, you know that right?" Evelyn says harshly.

"I know, but I'm happy with whatever he wants for us. I hope you'll be too." Angel now has tears from a different emotion roll down her soft cheeks.

"I will try to be." Evelyn puts her arm around Angel's shoulder. Mark still in the hall realizes his choices land on more than just himself.

I feel so much for Angel, she makes me feel like the world hasn't just ended. Why is it so hard to let myself feel for her? Why is it so hard to let myself feel anything? Maybe I can let myself go and just live in the now. Rachel even now, not alive, you're keeping me on my toes. All I can hear is you telling me to follow my heart. CLICK, CLICK, CLICK, CLICK, CLICK. Over the radio. Angel knowing what that means springs up and out to the main room

The radio keeps clicking as follows: one short, two long, one short, two short, two long, two short, two long, two short, one short, one long, three short, a pause, four short, one short, one short one long, one short, one short, then a long pause.

"What is that?" Mark asks

They all shush him. Angel closes her eyes to picture the letters, Chris is spelling on his hand. As the clicks start over the room begins to get smaller with anticipation.

"PIZZA'S HERE!" Ryan yells first. Looks of amazement fill the room then looks of fear in hopes the dead didn't hear the boy's yell. Chris moves to the window. Indeed, they did. The dead start to perk up and hunt for the source of the sound.

Angel keys the mic to respond "O.K." the clicks change pattern to spell out "30 tangos, moving on you." Angel answers with "orders". Only the word 'hold' comes across.

About two minutes pass and nothing comes on the radio, when suddenly loud classic rock blares in the distance. Sarge's voice comes over the radio, "Moving to you now."

Chris grabs the radio, "No! Sniper in the woods!" Before Chris even gets his words out the door swings open. In the haze of the bright light the large man fills the doorway. A bag slung over his back a rifle in his hand the glow of a cigar in his mouth.

He kicks the door closed behind him, "You only made it a day, and no sniper now. Did a sweep. Tracks coming in and going out on the far side of the lake. As for the Zeeks, they came from this side of the lake. A big moving truck, I think. The same way we get in and out." The strong voice of Sarge fills the main room, something that has been missed all day. "SIT REP" He looks at Angel

Angel begins, "Manny took one in the shoulder, he's out in the back. My big boy is in our cabin. Other than that, five by five sir." She says referring to her large caliber sniper rifle.

"Ok, here's the plan. We clear the Zeeks as they go for the boom box. Blades ONLY. Shoot only if you have too so we can draw them away as much as possible. Angel you get on the long gun, cover us on the way back." He sounds like the Sarge of old.

He puffs on the cigar and smoke fills the air. "Ex, you stay between us and her, so if either need help you respond. Mark you, Evelyn and I will take care of the Zeek problem." He hands them two long blades from his bag.

"I can help too, Sir!" Ryan says with a strong voice and even stronger jaw.

"This ain't kid stuff there boy. Killings gotta be done. No room for fear out there." Sarge looks down at the boy.

"I can do it. I can help." Ryan looks Sarge directly in the eyes. The look sends a chill through the room and up Sarge's spine.

"Mark, your call. We can use the help." Sarge looks to Mark, this partnership slowly reforming.

"Ryan, I love you..." Mark scans the room all eyes on him for the answer that could very well define a life. Knowing what words are coming next Ryan's eyes start to go to the ground. "Be safe. Sarge give him a blade he can handle."

You would think it was Christmas morning, his birthday, and the last day of school all at once by the joy that explodes out of the not so little boy, "I will dad."

The group has their orders they start out the door, with a 40-yard head start they have room to move free before the killing and danger starts.

Chapter:7 # Spook

Under an overcast sky, Sarge, Evelyn, Ryan, and Mark start down a narrow dirt pathway between two cabins. These cabins are smaller than Mark's, less refined as well. His has a front porch and resembles a normal house, these are more shack like. They give a spooky vibe, like the next slasher movie would be filmed in them. The path opens to a tree line, intermixed with tall and short trees. None have leaves this late in the fall. The smell of dead leaves replaces that of lake water. Winter weather is not far off. No one has kept perfect track of the days and months from the start, more picked it up based off Sarge's watch until it broke, but after that it was best guesses.

The crowd of Zeeks has moved on past the first set of trees and almost reached the boom box Sarge has hung in the corner of a pavilion. It is still pumping out the classic rock tunes. The pavilion is big, wide, and long. It fits twelve picnic tables under it, and the back is enclosed with a big stone fireplace that has no doubt hosted many fun birthdays, family reunions, and dinner dates. However now it is about to host an entirely different kind of gathering.

Sarge directs traffic, "Mark you and Ryan take left. Girl, you go right. I'm going middle, close them into that back wall. When I say the word back off, get away from here as quick as you can. We'll rendezvous back at the cabin. Angel and Chris should have our exit covered. Evelyn doesn't enjoy being called "girl" But it's an improvement over being called, "you".

Ryan and Mark circle to the left of the Pavilion, "Ryan, stay close but not too close. I'm going to slow them up you finish it, ok? If anything happens to me, you get to Sarge, if you can't get to him you run back to the cabin." Mark takes a few steps past Ryan.

Full of spirit, Ryan nods. The scene is set to a perfect 80's action movie complete with soundtrack. Evelyn is the first to record a kill in this fight. She's come a long way from being afraid of a phone ringing in the bathroom. She splits the Zeek's head transversely with one quick and targeted swing. As per-usual the first kill sparks something in the other Zeeks, they become more alert, more deadly.

The chilling shriek undoubtedly could be heard for miles. Sarge shuts that Zeek's eyes and mouth for good, with a spear like thrust of what looks like a Spartan sword. That goo-like substance sloshes out onto the concrete pad of the pavilion. The music is louder under the peaked roof. Hacking and whacking, Evelyn and Sarge back the Zeek army up on their sides. Meanwhile Ryan and Mark are going slow and have yet to record a kill.

Sarge seeing this jokingly says, "Ryan, I'm going to need you to pick up the pace."

Ryan, not taking it as a joke, pushes up to be arm and arm with his dad. Pride fills both Mark and Sarge. Ryan, being shorter, goes for the nearest Zeek's leg. SLICE! It drops to the ground teeth clacking trying to get to Ryan, to no avail. Ryan grabs his blade with both hands and with the mightiest thrust the young child can muster, he drives his machete blade through that Zeek's head, hitting the concrete underneath. Mark takes the moment in, not sure if its pride that fills him, but before he has a chance to say anything three Zeeks rush him.

With a judo like toss, one Zeek hits the ground. He reaches back to kill that one and another grabs his arm, teeth just inches from his wrist. Fear fills Mark for a second, he then feels the Zeek's weight shift and grip loosen. It falls to the ground. Ryan is there to save his father. Mark returns to the action killing the Zeek he'd tossed to the ground. Not having time to feel the relief well up inside.

The group has only killed a few, but most of the remaining are under the pavilion now, a few are still going for the Boom box. Sarge seeing how close they are to the backwall yells, "NOW! GO, GET OUT OF HERE!" He was the farthest inside the pavilion and has the tables blocking an escape from either side. Evelyn, Ryan, and Mark have made it away from the pavilion. Mark turns to find Sarge. Like the badass he is, Sarge is running out. He smiles and yells "PARTY'S OVER!" as he hits the edge of the concrete. BOOM! An explosion rushes out of the structure, Zeek body parts go flying. Sarge leaps out of the way. What is left of the roof collapses trapping or killing any Zeeks left inside.

"You wanted to be an action star, didn't you?" Evelyn jokes.

"Girl, I am an action star." Sarge brushes dirt off his pants.

Mark feels that calm wash over him again. They start the walk back. Evelyn and Ryan are in front by a few feet while Mark and Sarge seem to be walking slow with intent. Both men have something to say but neither one wants to start. Mark smiles at Evelyn giving Ryan a high-five and no doubt congratulating him on a job well-done.

Sarge grumbles, "The boy, he did good."

Mark takes a few more steps before responding, "Um, yeah. He did, didn't he?"

"Look Mark, about us… the things that happened…" Sarge trying to do the one thing he's not good at.

"Marlin, I know. You don't need to say anything. It was, however, good to see you having fun again." Mark says kicking a pebble.

They are back to the edge where the cabins start, "You and I are different, you know?" Sarge stops in his tracks.

Mark, not realizing Sarge has stopped keeps walking, "Yes, you're tough, and smart. I'm soft and kinda dumb." Mark jokes, only now seeing Sarge has stopped. "What is it, you see something?" Mark now alert scanning the area.

Sarge speaks soft "I do see something, a man just as good at what he does as I am. We lead in different ways. We provide different things, and I had a rough go at it when we got here. I'm a war hero, but things are peaceful, more often than not, until I go looking for a fight… and I always find one. Do you remember Doc? This is how we were." Sarge, remembering a friend who was lost at the start of this new death filled world. Another friend he wasn't there to save. "He was a lot like you, we butted heads just like this. I blamed you for him getting killed by that asshole. It ate at me. I wanted you to fill the void later. For both, I was wrong, you're you… I see it now. I think I even see what Angel sees too."

Mark was floored by how much Sarge said and didn't bark at all. He takes a few steps back toward Sarge, "I blamed myself for everyone we lost."

"That's the difference between good leaders and ok ones. A good one will blame themselves for anything first. The ok ones blame those around them. I lost that somewhere." Sarge puts his hand out to shake Mark's,

Mark gladly accepts. The two emerge from the woods, they are met by everyone but Manny and Grace. Chris hugs the men, neither one is thrilled about it. Angel jokes, "Bromance at its best." Chris lets go with a big smile on his face.

"Ok, that blast will draw the dead to us. I swept the area before to see what their numbers looked like. Didn't see anything we can't handle." Sarge sits at a picnic table.

"Where's Meg?" Mark looks around for her.

"She's out by the road in the truck." Sarge pulls out a map and lays it on the table. "Look at this." He begins to trace a shape on the map.

Sarge points out a big square around the lake and surrounding area. He's marked arrows pointing from where Dexter's house is, and the hotel. X's where they've encountered the dead. Blue question marks are on the far side of the lake. "I found this map. The hotel was already marked along with the x's. All the dick bag attacks have come from this side of the lake. Those Zeeks in the woods yesterday came from the far side. The tracks I've seen, someone covered almost well but again on the far side. I'm starting to think we have two fronts on this war."

Evelyn scans the group, "War? Like war, WAR?" She asks.

Mark puts his hand on her shoulder to comfort her. Angel making eye contact, "If we are, they have no idea the fire that will come for them girl." Angel strokes her rifle.

The gray dim natural light, from the wintery overcast sky seems as if even the world knows things are about to become darker. The water is still on the lake, acting as a mirror and making it appear the group is stuck between two storms.

Sarge puts his finger on the map. The far side has a Y road just at the edge. All other roads stop there. This is similar to the

cabin side of the lake. The lake only has cabins on one side. This helped to keep the cabins away from the noise and make for more seclusion. The group hasn't really gone over to the other side since it got cold. The beach is almost the entire bank of that side of the lake, sand at the water's edge and then a step up to a wooden boardwalk and dock. After the boardwalk a few wood buildings stand. One for snacks, one for souvenirs, the other is a game warden and service office. After that is a tree line of manmade landscaped trees and hills. The tree line is too straight to have grown naturally, the hills beyond that hide a parking field.

"Sarge, guess we're going to the beach?" Chris jokes.

"Be careful!" A voice calls from the background. The group turns to see who's speaking. Elsa is holding Manny around his waist.

Manny still without a shirt, blood-soaked bandage on his shoulder looks weak but he's alive. He takes labored steps down the stairs of the cabin. Elsa stops just before ground level. Manny holding his shoulder looking at everyone before him, "Thanks for not letting me die, but be careful, I think that's where the shot came from. I don't know who it was but if that's true, they may be just as good or maybe better than Angel."

Angel taking great offense at his words adjusts her rifle to her shoulder, "You want one in the other arm there, fucker?" All the fire and seriousness in her gray eyes.

"Angel, stop it." Mark semi-jokes. Angel looks at him like a cat, sad you took away their toy just before the fun started.

"We need eyes on. Angel, you find cover and get on overwatch. Mark, you, Chris, and I will go do recon. Ev, you keep a gun on that door. Hey you, small soldier, back her up." Sarge rolls the map up.

Evelyn looks welcoming to the orders from the grizzled man for the first time, maybe because he called her Ev, not Girl, or Evelyn, for the first time. She looks to him, "on it. Everyone else get inside. Let's get some food going so when they get back, we can have another family dinner." She says while pushing Ryan in the small of his back.

"Family dinner? What did I miss?" Sarge jokes.

"What bout Meg?" Chris askes.

"She's got her orders and a radio." Sarge checks the magazine in his rifle, handing his pistol to Evelyn, "Give this to the kid, keep them safe, girl." Sarge's eyes show a little light in a rare moment. Evelyn's eyes go back to piercing and sassy, "I missed you girl."

With that one short sentence Sarge melted Evelyn's heart, "Really?" She perks up her eyebrows. Sarge just smiles and turns away.

"Hey, old man... Watch your six!" Angel seeing the soft moment, looks both sad and glad at the same time.

"That's what I got you for daughter." Sarge smirks over his shoulder at her.

Mark, not one to let a possible goodbye slip away, hugs Evelyn, gives Ryan an air high five, since he's already on the porch of the cabin. Mark next to Angel, holds her hand and looks in her beautiful eyes. No words are spoken but the love language is received loud and clear. Their hands drift apart slowly as Mark steps away. In kind Chris and Evelyn are locked in a loving embrace. Their moment is caught in dead calm. A kiss separates the two.

"YO, Lover boys! Get the lead out and gear up." Sarge kills the rest of the calm.

Halfway to the far side of the lake, the men walk on. The path they could take is one that has been well worn in over years of kids and families seeking joy and fun. However, its exposed and that just won't do for a recon mission. Sarge has them walking in a small triangle, Chris at the point and Mark and himself in the back about twenty yards apart from each other. They walk in the hibernating trees. The trees groan as if they are warning them. A chill in the air hits Mark in the face, his eyes squint from it.

They stay silent on their approach. Slow purposeful steps guide them through the trees and to the edge where dirt and leaves turn to sand. They link up at the sand. Sarge instructs Mark to take the middle and Chris to take the boardwalk left, he will take the right, not many places to check and clear.

Chris, shotgun in hand starts looking in the window of the souvenir shop. Slowly opening the door, Sarge directs Mark to back Chris up. The door opens with a bell ringing. This shop with weathered and sunbeaten brown wood turned gray, is small in size. From the front door you can see to the back. When the group cleared it back in the summer they took all the fixtures from the sales floor and blocked the back-storage room with them so if they ever needed to use it as a hold up place or something of that nature the back would already be secure. In doing so they did not have to hope it was ready to defend. One quick sweep looking behind the sales counter and dressing rooms is all it takes, and they close the door behind them meeting up outside.

Next up is the office, this one they searched hoping for weapons or gear but all they found back then were maps and area attractions brochures. Sarge clears this one alone, as Mark and Chris keep watch outside. The tough man emerges out of the frontier like building. They move to the snack shop. This one is a harder to clear because it's two separate rooms. In front, it's just a counter to serve from with a roll up door, and warmer boxes with fast-food equipment. The back is just a small office, a big freezer and a breakroom, with a door to the outside. They chained the door so it could not be opened from the outside, that's the only door in or out of the structure. It is on the side of the building. Chris goes to check the lock. Mark and Sarge go to the roll up door, but it's ajar. The moment they notice it Chris whistles at them.

With a whisper he says, "The lock is cut, chain is gone."

All three pull their rifles to their shoulders, ready for the fight. With a slow count on his fingers Sarge counts to three.

As they snap the roll up door to its full up position. CLANK, CLANK, CLANK! The door rolls up.

Quickly the men scan with their barrels, no one is inside. What they do see is a big parabolic microphone and sound equipment, along with a tripod like a camera was set up.

"Whiskey, Tango, Foxtrot." Sarge is frozen by this discovery.

"I second that, what the fuck indeed?" Chris leans over the counter.

"Not sure but let's go in and see if we can find anything else." Mark takes charge. Mark and Chris round the corner and get ready to grab the doorknob.

Suddenly Sarge yells, "Stop don't open it!"

Both step back, asking why? Sarge jumps the counter and what seems like minutes go by, "Clear!" his voice comes through the door. With a blazing look Sarge says, "Door was rigged, claymore on a pull string."

"You think it was Dexter?" Mark asks.

"No, it doesn't make any sense, set up surveillance on us after he knew where we were? That's a waste of time just come in and kill us, with all the gear he had I don't think he'd be this covert about his movement. Besides he doesn't call the shots." Sarge's tactical brain is crunching the numbers to crack the mystery.

Chris calls from the small office, "Guys, you're gonna want to see this." Mark and Sarge rush over, "Ok, what's with the serial killer wall?" Chris points.

The wall is covered in pictures of the group, one side is a column of individual pictures of each person. Joey's has an X across it. Sarge and Meg have question marks on the bottoms of them. The others are just random shots of the group doing day to day things, some date back to the summer just after they'd gotten to the lake. They come across a note that says, "NO DOCTOR".

"Not a serial killer, this is a spec team's work. These are habit pictures, and the order of the pictures show leadership trickling down." Sarge reveals, now in overdrive almost spinning out of control.

"So why is my picture above yours Sarge?" Mark asks.

"Not sure but look, there are more pictures of you and Joey than anyone." Sarge points to the wall.

Chris who's been looking through papers on the desk, "He's right this looks like government file keeping, not the work of some backwoods rednecks. What the hell is this? Do you think...." Chris is silenced by a shush from Sarge.

"Listen, what is that?" Sarge closing his eyes to better use his ears, "It's a car, they're still here!"

The rumble of an engine gets louder as they rush outside, past the tree line and over the hill they run to the hidden parking lot, just in time to see a black SUV slinging dust behind it. As they flee with haste, they notice it has a low-profile satellite dish on top, blacked out widows and no license plate. On the door is a white outline of mountains. Sarge drops to a knee. POP, POP, POP. THWACK, THWACK, THWACK! His three shots hit the SUV, "Bulletproof, the thing's bulletproof." Sarge stands and grabs the walkie-talkie off his belt, "MEG! Black SUV coming your way remember what I told you." He speaks into it.

Chris and Mark look at each other, then to Sarge, "What's she doing?" Mark asks. He receives no answer just a look before Sarge takes off running. The unique sound of Sarge's truck rips through the trees. CRASH! The sound of two vehicles colliding then nothing, no sounds. Until shots ring out, BANG! BANG! POP, POP, BANG, POP, POP!

"THAT'S Meg! She's got them on the run!" Sarge smiles and picks up the pace.

They get to the wreck Sarge looks at his truck still on its wheels and little to no damage to it, but the heavy steel bumper pushed up a little, "MEG!" Sarge calls.

"Here." She pops out from behind Sarge's truck.

"You did good babe" Sarge kisses Meg, a good passionate kiss, "The devil is a woman, and she took a soul." Sarge says looking over the flipped SUV with pride.

The SUV is a smoking heap of twisted metal and glass, "There were four, maybe just three now." Meg informs them.

Rustling comes from the wreckage, guns fly to the ready as they investigate, a man is trying to pull himself out of where the windshield was, he has on a black tactical shirt with gray camo sleeves a patch of two mountain outlines on it, and black tactical pants, he reaches up for help. The man is gurgling. His hair is wet with blood, half his face is broken, eye almost shut, one last tug is all he had left, the life leaves the man... the gurgling stops.

They start to search the SUV for any information with little remorse, looking for something that would answer the many questions they now have. Sarge checks the man for ID, he finds a wallet with a few pictures in it, two kid's school pictures. They couldn't have been more than five and seven. No ID, no credit cards and nothing with a name on it.

"Got something!" Mark calls out. He holds a folder up its stamped with a Center for Disease Control federal seal.

"What is it Mark?" Chris says setting his shotgun down.

Sarge walks around to where Mark is, "It's a file about exposure, how people react and how long it takes. Looks like it's a breakdown of what to look out for. Like they are looking for signs of infection in us or something." Mark flips through page after page of this thick folder.

"Should we go after them? Or tell the others?" Meg asks.

"They're on foot. Can't get far and Angel will see'em with thermal well before they see her." Sarge spins his rifle to his back to climb in the SUV from the back window.

"Chris give me a hand getting this crate out of here." Sarge yells.

Mark still looking at papers, looks up at Meg getting back into Sarge's truck. He looks back down at the folder in his hands. Chris and Sarge are getting the black hard plastic box out of the SUV.

CRACK! The sound of a twig snapping grabs their attention. They look to where the sound came from, A voice calls from the back of Sarge's truck, "That's ours."

Another voice, this one female, "Thanks for getting it out for us."

Mark realizes he set his gun down to read the file. Chris has the same thought at about the same time. Both men are unarmed. Sarge still in the SUV, a place too tight to spin his rifle to get a shot off, reaches for his pistol he'd already given to Ryan.

Now another new voice, this one behind Sarge inside the SUV, "That easy, old man" the voice says. Sending a cold chill up Sarge's spine or maybe it's the gun barrel, "Drop it and get out slow." The man follows Sarge out at gunpoint.

Mark sees the man's face and can't help but feel it's familiar. His eyes are the most familiar to him, dark and showing almost no emotion. He stands just a bit taller than Sarge. He's comparable size wise, only younger and more fit. He has on the same uniform as the other person. No one moved to see the other two people holding them assumedly at gunpoint as well. The man at Sarge's back smiles and pokes Sarge with the gun to get him to step, only Sarge turns throwing an elbow at the man's head, the man ducks it as if it came in slow-motion. This man also moves out of the way of the next swing a right hook... Sarge is now off balance, the man simply puts his heel behind Sarge's and with just the tip of his pointer finger pushes Sarge to the ground. As he falls, Sarge's eyes get big and his face doesn't seem angry or worried that he's just been bested. He seems joyed. THUD! His body hits the ground.

"Now if I remember correctly, you owe me a beer and a lap dance? Not from you of course." The man smiles down on Sarge reaching out his hand to help him up.

Mark thinking, he must be an old trainee or something, feels relief. Chris turns to see the man behind him, who's lowered his weapon.

"So, does the bet still stand?" The man asks. He helps Sarge to his feet. They stand looking almost eye to eye, both reach to hug and a tattoo grabs Mark's attention. The man has a pink bird on his wrist, its playing with a soccer ball. The gears start to turn in his head. Before he can ask, his question is answered.

"Son, whatever you say. Just damn glad you're alive." Sarge grips him tight.

Chris is unsure of what's going on, "So are you going to kill us with the suspense now and not bullets?"

"Chris, Mark, this is Marlin, this is my boy. This is MJ." Joy fills Sarge as his words flow.

Floored they try and take it in, Mark not missing the reason they are all out here in the first place askes, "So if you knew him why'd you spy on us instead of just joining us?"

MJ responds in the most Sarge way possible, "Orders."

Sarge with no cares in the world at this moment, "Boy, my son. You look good."

"You look slow, I saw that elbow coming from miles away." MJ says with sarcasm.

"Maybe, maybe son. Angel is going to be so happy to see you." A tear rolls down the face of Sarge.

"Holy shit! I thought your tear ducts were welded shut!" Chris jokes.

Meg out of the truck, moves to Sarge. The other woman has yet to show herself and this is unsettling to Mark. He looks back for her again, "So, you know who we are, who are you?"

"Quinn, show yourself, I think you're making Mark uncomfortable." MJ calls out.

"Jeez, he's always uncomfortable." Her voice gets closer. Mark sees her finally. Same gear as the other two, black shirt with gray camo and black pants. She doesn't seem like a fighter, not like Angel who looks like she'd kill you just as soon as look at you.

"Let's get into this back at your cabin seeing as you just flipped our house." MJ jokes.

"Of course, grab your gear and toss it in the back of my truck and we'll go." Sarge walks with his arm around MJ.

"I have to admit, I didn't see the truck thing coming." MJ smiles in compliment, "Dallas, go grab anything you need from the outlook." MJ sends the other man away. The man disappears like a shadow.

"What about your guy here that's passed?" Chris looks down at the poor mangled man a small amount of sadness in his face.

"Quinn knows what to do." MJ disappears behind the truck.

Chris whispers to Mark, "His son, the gay one?" Mark cuts Chris a look. They turn and watch.

Quinn pulls a yellow bottle out of her gear bag. Squirts it all over the body and tosses a match, the body ignites. She says words that can't be heard and walks away.

Mark still unsure of the entire situation, "Yeah, I guess. I only think he has two kids. This is still fishy to me." Mark and Chris elect to sit in the bed of the pickup truck. The ride back isn't very long and not much is said.

The truck pulls up the drive to the cabin, headlights illuminating the dust kicked up by the tires. The night is setting in and the temperature dropping quickly.

Sarge hops out first, MJ and Quinn slide out of the back door of the quad cab truck. The cabin is dark and quiet. The air is cold and crisp as it whips off the lake. Sarge puts his hands to his mouth "Ev, it's us!" he calls out. The door to the cabin slowly opens. The glow of a lantern brightens the doorway.

"Dad?" Evelyn's voce calls out.

"Yeah Ev, it's us, we're ok." Mark says climbing out of the truck.

Quinn and MJ round the truck to grab the gear they retrieved from the wreckage. Mark and Chris scan the area for Angel. Sarge, still overjoyed, seems to be almost skipping as the group starts towards the cabin. Quinn looks at the bullet strikes on the exterior of the cabin.

"You guys got lucky it was during our routine check in. If we didn't step in, you'd have suffered more casualties." Quinn enters the cabin setting eyes on a table full of food.

MJ is next through the door, "Yeah, sorry about that. I was going for the door and Manny... You opened it at the worst time."

Manny sitting in an armchair looks up at MJ "He shot me? Who the hell is this guy...? He's so tall." Manny starts to giggle.

"Sorry, he's kind of high on pain meds." Elsa explains.

Sarge, the last in line, is now in the cabin, "Everyone, this is Marlin Jr. and his associate, Quinn. This is my son." Sarge smiling big.

Evelyn floored now, "First he has a daughter, now a son? I'm so confused."

"Don't worry, it wears off." Chris smirks, hugging Evelyn.

Sarge pulls out the radio and smiles as he keys the mic, "Angel, shut it down."

A quick click over the radio, "Roger. On my way."

"She's going to lose her shit." Sarge sits on the couch.

Meg takes a seat at the dinner table facing the door. MJ, Quinn and Mark all continue standing in the kitchen, Chris and Evelyn are getting a fire going.

They can all hear the boot steps up the front stairs, they seem to be falling in what feels like minutes apart. One after the other. THUD! THUD! THUD! The doorknob starts to turn. Everyone in the room is still except MJ, his steps match those coming from outside. He stands at the door waiting for it to open.

Angel pushes the door open looking down at the last step up into the cabin, MJ takes one step closer. That would prove to be one too many. As Angel lays eyes on her brother for the first time since he left her all those years ago, a rage fills her. The sound of fist hitting flesh is the only greeting she gives.

Angel unloads on MJ, punch after punch. Backing him up to the dinner table. The chairs and dishes clang together, he uses the table to catch himself. A strong left hook drops him to the ground. Blood spewing from his face. The room looks on in horror as she mounts him and punches until her arms grow heavy. Tears running down her cheeks, "How could you, how could you, HOW COULD YOU?!" she cries.

Mark broken free from the stunning events drops to a knee and wraps his arms around Angel, "Angel stop, I got you, stop." He pulls her off.

Angel bursts out into the night, fists bloody and eyes full of hurt, MJ a bloody mess on the ground, the room full of on lookers.

Mark takes off after her, knowing if given enough time and if she didn't want him to, he'd never find her again. He looks around in the fleeting light, scanning the immediate area. The sound of the breeze in the dead leaves sounds like a thousand rattle snakes all around him. A few more steps and he can hear a faint voice. Sitting on the ground by the edge of the lake Angel appears.

"Angel, its me." Mark says softly so as not to end up her next target.

"I know dumbass, just come sit down already." She snarks.

Mark does just that, he sits on the cold damp shoreline next to her. He doesn't reach for her, instead he just sits in silence with her. Angel, appreciates what Mark is doing, showing her love in the way she understands. She reaches for the hand propping him up, placing hers partially on his.

"Mark, he… He was dead to me for so long. I buried him in a box in my head and fought the urge to visit that grave." She looks out over the water, the small ripples catching the light.

Mark unsure of what to say, inches closer to her. Now they are shoulder to shoulder, "He didn't even tell me goodbye, he told Sarge whatever and was gone. I don't feel bad for what I did to that dead man, not one bit." Anger wells up in her voice.

"Angel, I'm not going to tell you how to react to this, but I think you at least owe him the chance to explain." Mark pulls Angel to his chest.

Accepting his affection, she closes her eyes taking in the moment, "Mark, can you do something for me." She asks eyes shut tight.

"Anything, of course." He replies.

"Can you call me by my real name just once? I want to hear it from someone I love before I hear it from his voice." She grips him a little tighter.

Without time to process that she said she loves him, "Sure, but I don't even… I don't know what it is." Mark suddenly sees how far away she's kept him all this time.

"My name… my… its Abigail." She says this as if a heavy weight has been lifted off her.

Mark smiles, feeling as if he was just told the biggest secret in the world, "Abigail? Ab-i-gail, Abi or Gail?" Mark looks down at her.

"Oh my God, stop." Angel smiles and sits back up looking into Mark's eyes.

Looking back at her, "Abigail, kiss me." In this moment nothing matters, not the age difference, not the loss of a wife, nor the return of a brother. The only thing that matters in this moment is the connection of these two hearts, when this moment ends the world begins again.

Mark pulls away first, "Can we get up now? My butt is soaking wet." He laughs.

"Yeah, let's go. DON'T say a word about my name or I will cut you!" Angel pokes him in the side. He giggles and squirms away from the poke.

"Ok, ok, ok, got it." Mark starts to walk back to the cabin. Angel is a few steps behind him. She's looking at the lake and the spot where they sat taking a mental picture.

Chapter:8 What Had Happened Was

The cabin is aglow with just the kitchen light on. The fireplace, warming the room, gives off a pleasant smell as Mark opens the door. He is met by Quinn, MJ, Sarge, Chris and Elsa at the table, "What's going on?" Mark can feel the bad energy in the room.

Sitting at the table under the small pendent light Quinn looks to Mark, "Sarge wants to understand why we're here. Since your gal pal there almost broke his jaw, I'm doing the talking." She looks past Mark right at Angel entering the cabin behind him.

Angel not interested in another fight stops in her tracks, "Sweetheart if you wanna keep talking, you should put your eyes back in your fucking head."

"Oh, that's right, everyone's supposed to be afraid of you." Quinn slides back in her chair making room to get up if need be.

Angel, still just inside the doorway, smiles, "You can be whatever you want to be just be that shit over there." Angel folds her arms.

Quinn seemingly trying to get a rise out of Angel, "It's easy to sound tough from across a room," She looks at MJ, "And it's easy to beat someone who didn't want to fight. You think you're the baddest chick in the apocalypse? Trust I would wreck you and your Marine training." Quinn says smugly.

"ENOUGH!" Sarge's booming voice silences them both, "As much as I'd love to see Angel defend the Corps. As fun as that would be it won't get us anywhere." Neither woman seems happy about being talked to that way.

In a mumble MJ Speaks, "He's right, we are on the same side." He holds his jaw after talking.

Angel looks at MJ, eyes still filled with rage, "I'll go keep watch." Anger and resentment coat her words, as she reaches for her rifle and not Mark.

Unsure what to do Mark lets her leave without a word or an action on his part. He walks to the table picking up a glass of water from in front of Chris, "Ok so let's hear it." Mark sits at the table across from Quinn, his back to the door.

Quinn looks at MJ for the go ahead, he pushes a blue file folder across to her, "So when this started, we had no clue what it would be. The thing you have to understand is we didn't think the dead were going to walk, death and hysteria, yes we expected that. When I say 'We' I mean the United States." She flips the folder open, on the inside a picture of Dr. Gibson paperclipped to it, the top page is a Memo stamped COPY in big letters. She starts to read it, "Dr. Gibson has tested his device, we are confident in its ability to be an asset picking up viral saturated air. It is at our recommendation, that you move forward with his research. We will await further instructions on this matter." She flips the page over, looking at MJ for more approval. "That was dated April 12th, 2013, we received no information back." She looks down at the next page and begins to read again, "We have had repeated positive tests out of the Midwest airports, specifically Chicago O'Hare, Denver International, Des Moines International, and Dallas/Fort Worth International. The threat is growing every day. We are, at this point still unsure what the virus is or aimed to do. We will continue to report and update you as we know more."

Sarge is becoming restless, this is off putting to Mark and Chris, "I don't understand what that means." Chris looks at the faces around the table.

"This is what he was doing. Dr. Gibson, he said he was in contact with the CDC." Sarge seems angry.

"Yes, and he thought he was. It didn't seem to be important enough." Quinn says flipping the page, "That was dated April 19th, 2013, he sent one almost every week for the next month, but no one wanted to deal with it. Not the CDC, not POTUS, not the people that even tasked him to move forward with his work." Quinn cuts her eyes to Sarge, she seems almost sad.

Mark sifting through the information, vague as it may be, "So what, we could have stopped this? I don't think so. Dr. Gibson didn't even really understand it."

Quinn looks back at the folder now it looks like a printout of emails, "He didn't until he did what any good researcher does. He started to reach out to the scientific community. Everyone laughed at him... until he received an email from an encrypted account. This was the conversation between he and a person that went by EB, the Doctor started." She starts to read, "Hi, I'm hoping to find anyone that will act. I believe we are under attack."

MJ stops her, "This is where it got interesting."

Quinn goes on to read, "Hi, Doctor. Can you explain your findings to me?" Quinn stops looking at the papers and turns her gaze to the group of on lookers, "He went on to explain what he'd found and where he was. They went on and on, it almost became a romantic relationship. This EB had finally put this on the map and Dr. Gibson felt accepted for once."

"Bullshit, no way. He said he was being instructed on all of this not the other way around." Sarge starts to unleash his fury.

"I understand but realize this was not what we intended either." MJ mutters to his father.

Mark, getting a vision of who EB could have been, "So this EB... she work for anyone?" He asks a pointed question.

Quinn, seeing that Mark is piecing the parts together, "Yes she got an approval by the Joint Chiefs and the President himself... she started a field lab. This lab, it was set within driving distance of the doctor's location."

"You have got to be kidding me?" Mark now understanding Sarge's rage, "The T.O.B. EB, Emily Berg." Mark remembers the doctor in charge at the temporary operating base. "But they acted like they didn't know each other when we met."

"It wasn't an act. She wasn't sure it was really him until she pulled your information to see if you two were who you said you were. This lady was a nutjob and it wouldn't surprise me if she thought she made the entire conversation up in her head." Quinn looks back to the paper, "EB responded, 'I've got it. They are letting me investigate in the field. The rise in violence in the affected areas has made the higher ups nervous!' she said. After they discussed the symptoms a bit, then she told him to come find her at her field lab." Quinn closes the folder, "Understand, this lady was crazy. She had worked her entire career to be the one to stop something exactly like this. So, when she had her shot, she took it."

Chris stands and starts to walk away, "This is beyond me, I hated playing clue as a kid. I'm going to go see how Evelyn and the kids are doing." He walks down the hall.

MJ, is looking at Sarge as they turn back to the conversation, "And that's when we lost you." He hangs his head in shame.

Sarge is confused, "Lost who? How?"

"How do you think an asshole low rent security operator got such a high-profile gig?" Quinn sits back in her seat.

MJ, eyes still at the ground, "It was my first assignment as lead. Protect this crazy doctor. He isn't important so don't pull a tier 1 asset, put a private organization on it, they told me."

Mark stunned, "Wait, you put them with Dr. Gibson?"

"Yes, I had to be able to trust the team. I'd been keeping tabs on my dad and sister for some time at that point. He had just come off a big job so I knew they would allow it. His team was still green but had an amazing background." MJ still hasn't looked up.

Sarge now filled with emotion exclaims, "Keeping tabs? How long?"

"Shortly after I left." MJ reveals.

With pain in his voice Sarge asks just one question, "You didn't leave out of fear of acceptance, did you?"

"Dad, you have to understand. They came to me with an offer of everything you had trained me for. The cost was no connections, nothing that could be used against me…" MJ pleads.

Sarge pushes himself away from the table so hard the entire table almost flips, "For years, YEARS! I hated myself. I shut your sister out for a long time because of you." Sarge storms out of the cabin.

Mark is left to sift through the wreckage. Quinn gets up and fills a cup of water. The shadowy cabin now somber as well, feels empty. As she puts the cup to her lips to drink Mark looks away back to the fire.

"When you say you lost them, what did you mean?" Mark says staring at the licks of the flames in the fireplace.

With disgust MJ responds, "We were tracking them, but all hell broke loose and then the government lost its mind and turned it's guns to civilians."

Quinn places her hand on MJ's shoulder, "It wasn't your fault." She comforts him.

Mark seeing this backs off, "When you left, was it because you didn't feel accepted or was it because you thought it would make him hate you if you were?"

"If you're asking me if I'm really into dudes, yes I am. I had a secret boyfriend at that time but nothing is a secret from that man… he knew." He says with grit in his voice.

Mark picking up on the touchy subject tries to soften his next question, "I mean, did you really think he was going to hate you for it?"

"I told him the truth he didn't want to see back then, the agency told me I had to distance myself from family and that man, he never did well with the truth." MJ seems almost angry.

Mark gets up from the table asking Elsa if she needs anything because she's been all but forgotten with all the bombs dropping around them.

Elsa has remained silent during this entire ordeal. A trait that has kept her safe. She isn't a fighter and before she was a teller at a small bank. Her skill set is geared to calm and efficient, often keeping an eye on things but not saying much. This subject hasn't been very different until, "No, thank you Mark, I am new to all of this. I've only heard the stories of what happened in the city. This all sounds like fate to me." Elsa gets up from the table, "I'm going to go check on Manny, good night everyone."

After Elsa's exit Mark goes to the window and looks out into the darkness. The window didn't shatter completely from the gunshot, just a corner that they've since patched. His thoughts are on Angel more than anything, hoping she's ok and not in a tree somewhere head cloudy. Quinn and MJ are talking behind him but he's unable to make out all the words, but he picks up Dallas's name. This jars him realizing MJ sent him away hours ago and he'd never returned.

"Where is he." Mark turns to look at them both.

MJ Seems confused, "Who? My father?"

Mark displeased knowing full well what MJ is up to, having seen Sarge do it countless times before, "Dallas. You sent him off. Shouldn't he have been back by now?"

Quinn steps in, "That's what we were talking about, He hasn't reported in either."

Mark fighting the thoughts on distrust reaches for his radio to call for Angel, asking for a check in. She responds with an all clear. Mark keys the mic, "Sarge I know you have your ears on, I have a weird feeling stay close."

Quinn picks up her gear bag and moves to the door. Mark looks at her but knows he can do nothing to stop her. Like vapor she vanishes into the night. Mark and MJ are the only ones in the main room now.

 "So, MJ you've been on this from the start?" Mark says continuing to look out at the darkness as if it was looking back at him.

MJ manipulating his jaw makes a yep sound followed by, "I guess, didn't know this was the way it'd play out."

"I was out here when it started, taking in this same view. Kids distracted, but me... my mind was still on the important things." Mark smiles a bit. "I never knew what happened really, how fast it spread, that sort of thing. Being out here we didn't even know till we got back to the city." Mark walks back to the table, his steps soft and almost ghost-like. He does not sit, however.

MJ looks up at him, "It happened like any pandemic. By the time anyone wanted to hear about it. It was too late. There was so much we didn't know or understand at that point." MJ's face reads of failure.

Mark asks a few questions, about the start. He walks around as he receives his answers.

MJ opens a folder different from the other that had the information about Dr. Gibson, "The first hot zone wasn't clear, we didn't really have a ground zero. The first spike was only 12 people. Then cases started to spread between Illinois, Iowa, Missouri, Kansas, and Nebraska. No one listened to us. And why should they? Green agent put on a job no one wanted, but soon they had no choice. We didn't shut down the airports quick enough. Before we knew it, cases went from 12 to 48 in four days and more cases spread over more states. Then we saw the big picture, Colorado, Oklahoma, and Texas all had cases. Too much ground to cover that fast." MJ flips the page in the folder, he reads a line, "We have reason to believe this was a deliberate biological attack, please advise."

Mark stops in his tracks "Who sent that?"

MJ flips the page once more, "I did. My director never responded. After that I did what the orders of the operation were. We watched and took notes. In just 7 days we had 4,000 cases across the mid-west. That's when the CDC took notice. Asking for our notes and telling us to stand down and turn the operation over to them and their taskforce. That was July 1st, I refused to do anything until I was given the order from my director because that's who I reported to. On the 2nd I got a phone call from the Surgeon General, telling me I was to brief the President of the United States direct. So, I did. On the 3rd we had reported 192,000 cases. Emily had so many crazy theories like canine DNA, that somehow it was involved. She wasted any extra time we had on nonsense."

Mark not following the tracking of the sickness, "How did you track the cases?"

"We didn't have a test it was just people coming in for related symptoms, vertigo, stiffness, and pain. It was people being treated for more migraines, and others with tremors. Once we knew what to look for, we started seeing the patterns. Like the rise in homicides in the affected areas. Unfortunately, by then it was too late for us all." MJ closes the folder on the table.

Mark looks down the hall with thoughts of his kids, "So, why are we still alive?"

"Not sure really. This thing is unlike anything we've ever seen. It is MS, that part we know but it works alongside something else that has yet to be understood. It's that thing that kills the body as the MS attacks your brain stem. Research says healthy lifestyle can keep MS at bay. Maybe it's something that some people have a natural immunity to, maybe not, I don't know. That's the part we needed the doctor and his research for, but when we lost him. We lost so much. Epidemiologist broke down what they could, but we lost so much time. I was of little help." MJ points out he wasn't a scientist. Mark seems to not fully trust the information evident by the ruffle in his brow.

The fire behind the two of them pops and hisses as it burns out, their attention is grabbed by Mark's radio and a frantic Angel.

"What is it?" Mark answers.

"We have multiple waves of Zeeks incoming too many to count." She informs him.

Mark and MJ spring to action. Mark calls to the others down the hall, "Get up, get up! We have a fight coming!"

Over the radio he calls for Sarge but receives no response. He tries Angel, "Angel, are you on your way here?"

The radio clicks but it takes her a moment to speak, "They are on me, I'm trapped. Mark there are so many."

"ANGEL! ANGEL!" Mark yells, but no response. He runs to the door, "I'm going to get her." But before he makes it out of the door Chris's hand grabs him.

"Boss we need ya, on this side not theirs. Don't go rushing to your death now."

Mark calms himself. Evelyn emerges from the hall gun at the ready. Chris tells her to get Elsa and kill the lights everywhere. Like a flash she takes to the task. The Zeeks must still be a ways off because they can't hear their symphony of horror yet.

"Can you get Quinn back?" Mark asks opening the door.

MJ closing the straps on his tactical vest and gear answers, "No, if she can see what's going on or is still looking for Dallas, she's radio silent and wouldn't respond." Such cold reactions from MJ and his team jar Mark.

Chris is loading up a pouch with as many shotgun shells as will fit. Evelyn returns, hair in a ponytail ready for action. The four stand at the door. Elsa slowly walks to the main room dread on her face. Mark instructs her to guard the cabin and stay on the steps. She still seems uncomfortable having to fight. However, in this world you are not afforded that luxury, so fight she must. She is the last line of defense for the kids and the still recovering Manny.

"I'm missing Joey right about now." Chris says surveying the area around the cabin as they begin their descent into battle.

Mark, struck with sadness stops in his tracks. His thoughts are jumbled, his vision blurs. A bright light is in his face, as he tries to raise his hand to block the light he can feel his arm being held back. MJ's voice calls to him. At first it sounds extremely close, then like its down a hallway.

"Mark, snap out of it. Mark keep going." MJ commands.

The bright light is gone Mark looks at his arm seeing MJ holding it, "Sorry, I'm not sure what that was."

MJ releases Mark's arm, "We need to move. I'm not seeing anything yet."

Mark, MJ, Evelyn, and Chris are on the move looking for the first wave of Zeeks. Now 200 yards into the woods on this cold and calm night, the moon hides behind clouds only giving quick flashes of light. The direction they went is towards the main road, that's the only place they know Angel has a tree stand.

She's got more than one but being her, she keeps the location to herself to preserve her alone time.

MJ has tried to fall to the back of the asymmetrical line, Chris wouldn't let it happen. Evelyn waves to get someone's attention, she points to one Zeek zig zagging between the trees. The group doesn't run into the fast movers still in the early stage of the virus much anymore. They see the late stage slow and dimwitted ones most often. MJ draws his knife and stalks the Zeek. As he makes his move sinking his knife into its head, he realizes they have walked right into the middle somehow.

"MARK, BEHIND YOU!" MJ yells.

One Zeek has turned to a dozen and more on the way. BOOM! Chris's shot shatters the quiet night. Now a cascade of gun fire cutting throughout the woods. Every shot seems like a magnet drawing more and more Zeeks.

Evelyn has stayed close to Chris. She calls out, "I'm almost empty!" she's gone through any extra she brought with her. Mark is also out of ammunition.

MJ and Chris are still firing, MJ is down to his pistol that is also low on ammunition, "Everyone on ME!" Chris yells.

They follow the order, "We need to fall back there are too many to keep going this way." Chris covers the retreat.

They make their way back to the cabin. Even in the cold, sweat is running down their faces. Covered in blood spatter they emerge out of the woods shocking Elsa.

"Oh my!" she gasps.

The feeling of defeat washes over them, knowing they'll have to go back out and quickly. Mark tries Sarge over the radio again, "Sarge we could really use you right now. Too many

Zeeks to fight off." Mark noticing the fear on Evelyn's face makes a decision, "Ev, go get Meg. Swap with her keep your brother and the others safe."

Evelyn unsure why he's telling her this responds, "Dad, I can help." She tries to sound strong.

Chris backs Mark up, "Ev, I think we need to know this place is safe if we need to fall back again. No one I'd rather run home to than you." He says with love in his eyes.

MJ scans the area, "Guns aren't enough. Do you have any axes, bats, hell anything bigger than a knife?" He asks realizing he was never equipped for a large-scale fight.

Chris is quick to answer, "We got one ax we use for firewood, a bat and an old croquet mallet." Chris motions to where each can be found.

Meg has made her way outside. She looks just as afraid as Evelyn, but she is handling things better than back when this all started. Her time with Sarge has awakened her inner badass in some ways. She looks to Mark for direction, like she would have back before when she was Marks office manager. However, now things are more severe than who to call for ordering more office supplies.

"Mark, where do you need me?" Meg asks with very little wobble in her voice.

Mark has picked up the croquet mallet, taking a few swings. In the dark it's hard to see its motion, but the two white ends create almost a glowing arc, "Keep behind us. Anything we knock down, you make sure it stays down, ok?"

"Ok, boys and girl... let's get to it." MJ leads the way.

On the trek back to the battle grounds the group is stealthy and spread out in almost a V formation with MJ at the point, Chris to his left, Mark to his right, and Meg a few yards behind. The sound of the Zeeks is getting louder. MJ directs them to stop while he plots an attack strategy.

Chris has seen something MJ has clearly missed, he aggressively points to his left and whispers, "Psst, eyes on."

Mark scans the darkness to pick up whatever Chris is seeing, "Angel?" He asks.

MJ has zeroed in on what Chris is looking at, "50 yards, single tree, looks like they got something pinned, not sure if it's her or not."

Finally, Mark sees the group, "What's the plan here?" He asks looking at the ever-moving circle of hands and teeth.

"They're distracted. We can hit them from behind. Chris you push the left back. I'll clear the center, and Mark, Meg, keep us from getting surrounded." MJ delegates.

They sneak up on the group, as the fighting starts MJ engages first. With a crack of the bat Zeeks start hitting the ground. Chris gets a running start and puts momentum behind his first swing, that comes from high to low. THUCK! The ax lands deep in a younger looking Zeek's head. Chris puts his boot on the Zeek's shoulder to unbury the ax. Meanwhile behind him MJ has put three Zeeks on the ground. Meg and Mark arrive on the scene, Mark can't help but look up to see if Angel is up there. Upon looking up he is shocked to see Angel holding a gun to her head.

"Angel, WE'RE HERE! NO!" He yells with all the passion and fire to instantly grab her attention even over all the noise from the undead crowd around him.

"Mark?" She asks to the darkness, looking down to see him, "Mark, LOOK OUT!" she yells.

Mark brings his gaze to ground level and is met with fingers and teeth. He manages to use the croquet mallet to push the Zeek back. The Zeek lets out a devilish snarl, Mark swings the mallet with all his might. CRACK! The head of the light and now seemingly flimsy backyard toy snaps off and flies into the night.

Mark, at a loss looks at this undeterred Zeek, "Sorry," He says taking a few steps back. Just then his heel catches a tree root, and he slams to the ground. This practically serves him up on a platter. The Zeek instinctually drops to the ground savoring the meal almost at its grasp. BANG! A loud shot and the Zeeks body hits the ground.

"Get up dummy!" Angel calls, "You're here to save me remember?"

Mark, realizing he only has the handle of the mallet now, looks at where the head broke off. It left a point. Mark puts the leather lanyard around his wrist and wraps his hand around the now three-foot-long spear, his grip tight and eyes focused. With several strong and sharp thrusts, he has found a pace he can keep up with.

Zeeks are hitting the ground faster than they're appearing now. The living has the upper hand. Just a few Zeeks remain, its safe for Angel to climb down from the tree stand. Upon doing so she gets to the ground. One slow moving and rather stupid Zeek limps and hobbles its way towards her, that is the last thing it does. Thunk! She crushes it's head in with the butt of her rifle.

Not one to miss an opportunity to make a joke Chris says, "We done now?"

"Yeah, let's get home." Mark smiles.

"You guys go I'm going to take the long way back, see if I run into Sarge, Quinn, Or Dallas." MJ wipes the fight from his face.

"So, send more people to find the other people that went looking for the first missing person, sounds smart." Meg says turning to walk away.

"Be safe and smart. I still have questions for you, so you better come back." Mark says.

MJ looks at Angel, "I'm glad we got to you in time... I still love you... for what it's worth" MJ says.

"Eat shit." Angel snaps.

"Angel!" Mark says with a trace amount of laughter in his voice.

MJ smiles, "It's ok." MJ walks off disappearing.

Mark addresses something important, "Angel what was that back there? You don't care if you die now?"

"I care but looking down at them I couldn't help but see all the living people I've killed, coming to serve justice on me."

Mark devastated by a look in her eyes, reaches for her hand, "Whatever you did, that's in the past... we need to look to the future. I want you in mine."

Now on the slow-paced walk back to the cabin the events of the night start to replay for Mark, "Hey, Meg? What did you mean back there?"

"Back where?" She responds.

"You said 'send more people to go look for the first person that went missing' do you know what Sarge is up to?" Mark questions.

"He, he went to search for Dallas and back to the other side of the lake to see what else he could find, something isn't sitting right with him." Meg shares.

"I knew it!" Chris yells.

Chapter:9 Fathers and Sons

The group arrives back at the cabin, eager to put the long night to rest, they all retreat to their rooms, all but Mark.

Rest would not come until he knows Sarge is safe. He sits on the steps of the cabin thinking to himself as the cold nips at his neck and fingers. *I can't believe how crazy this day was. We've been here for months now and have never seen anything like today. MJ saving us and blowing their cover. Whoever it is bringing the fight to our door. What could they possibly want? I guess just death and destruction. Rachel, I miss you. You'd know what to say to calm my anxious mind. I hate myself for falling for Angel, and still thinking of you. She's younger than me in what should be a weird way, but she's lived differently. In a way that aged her soul. Rach, I can hear you now making fun of me 'What trading me in for a younger model? Hope you get the warranty because they don't make them how they used to.' Laughing your sweet, sexy laugh. Even still I can't help but be drawn to her. Ev, has given me so much these last few days, you would be proud of her, she has your fire and fearlessness, and Ryan. He is fighting for my attention. I want to give it to him, but everything is so crazy. I just want to keep him safe but that kid, that kid can take care of himself. You did good with them my love, the best Mom they could have ever had.*

Mark is startled, the feeling of cold water snaps him awake. He opens his eyes to Sarge. Mark is completely dry, but still just as alarmed. He fell asleep on the steps outside.

"Hey Mark, you know when you keep watch you're intended to stay awake right?" Sarge jokes.

Mark groggy laughs sarcastically. He slides down so Sarge can sit, "You find what you were looking for last night?"

"Na, I didn't find anything. I think I'm just over thinking it. MJ is blood, he's my blood." Sarge hands Mark a cup of coffee.

As he sips his own, both men look out over the lake, steam rising off the liquid in the cold morning air. They sit in silence for a few minutes, sitting in peace for the first time in what seems like weeks, the sun at their backs.

"Do you think if we'd met under different circumstances, we'd be friends?" Mark asks.

With a laugh, Sarge responds, "Hell no."

With a chuckle back Mark says, "Fair enough, jerk."

Sarge smiles and goes back to sipping his coffee. He seems more at peace than he ever has, "What should we do today?"

"It's getting cold, and snow isn't far. We need to stock up on wood." Mark puts his cup down.

Just then the door opens Angel's voice, "Sorry, am I interrupting something?"

"Actually!" Mark says standing to look at her.

"I was wondering where you were, you never came to bed last night." Angel stepping aside for him.

Sarge uncomfortable says "And that's my cue..." He pushes past Mark jokingly, "Meg awake?" He asks Angel.

"No, she's here on the couch asleep still." Angel lets him past.

Sarge walks to Meg, he kisses her softly.

Mark heads to the kitchen to look at the empty fridge and cabinets, "Sarge, we may need to make a food run. With all this stuff going on we haven't been out in a while I guess."

"Ok we'll put Ex and the girl on it." Sarge replies.

Evelyn appears in the living room from the hall, "The girl? I had a name for a whole twenty minutes with you?" She jokes.

The group gathers one by one to talk over the day's goals. This time it's simple and has a togetherness that's been vacant for so long. Chris and Evelyn will go on a run for food, Elsa and Manny will take stock on what they have and get back to keeping track of what they use. Mark and Sarge will hang out around the cabin cutting wood and trading off keeping watch. Angel elected to treat the water so they can have plenty of good drinking water.

As they ready themselves to get started MJ and his crew come through the door.

"Well, look what the cat dragged in!" Chris says.

"Long night for everyone." MJ says pulling out a chair at the table.

Sarge gets up from his seat, "See you found your man, good."

"Yeah, I was pinned between here and the wreck. I just dug in and waited it out. Till Quinn found me and MJ found us." Dallas explains, "Glad, you guys made it through the deadies. From what MJ said it was a lot of them."

Quinn cuts through the pleasantries, "You look like you were on your way out, what's up?" She's put herself between the door and everyone else.

"Supplies and getting things back on track." Mark says.

Quinn's tune changes, "Oh, good we can show you a few places we've scouted but never had a reason to try and hit."

Chris speaks up having been one of the ones scouting for supplies, "Really? How far out?"

Dallas backs her up, "Not far, one is a homeless shelter, and another was a church that took over a decent sized farmhouse. They ran both the shelter and the church to help the homeless and battered women."

"How the hell do you know about those?" Manny askes.

MJ sensing the skepticism, "Look, we did our homework before getting here. We did research on the area just in case. When we first got here, we didn't know how long we'd be here and had to have a plan in case we got split up or something."

Mark tries to also keep the peace, "Come on guys sounds like places we'd have never noticed or would look past because we didn't know what they were."

MJ and Sarge speak at the same time, "Exactly" they say in unison.

Quinn moves from the door, "Dallas and I will show you. Who was going out? Chris, I assume?"

"I understand you've been watching us for who knows how long, but if you can stop with the creepy insights on us, I'd appreciate it." Chris says, "Evelyn, and I were going."

Dallas smiles, "Got it Tex."

MJ, Sarge, and Mark all agree on the plan for the day. The two groups seem to have found a working relationship, at least for the time being. Chris has even seemed to lighten up on them in the time before they leave the cabin to go on the search for supplies. Sarge and MJ seem to laugh more when they talk now.

Angel is keeping her distance, but most likely for MJ's safety than anything else.

Outside now, saying goodbyes, unlike in times past when someone you know and love heads out to go run an errand, it is way more of a production. Before you say bye and move now, it is hugs and long winded 'be safe and I love yous'. The sky is overcast like it is much of the winter. Clouds looks like rolling waves, the sun finding little pinholes to shine through like spotlights from beyond. The morning is very cold, so cold the ground seems like concrete that just a few days ago was soft enough to leave footprints in. No wind makes it livable to be outside, but you can still see everyone's breath and tell the cold is slowly cutting into them.

Mark hugs Evelyn hard and tight, like a father sending his kid off to college. However, the education she could get out there will not be something you earn a degree from but rather knowledge that could keep you alive, or get you killed.

"Be smart out there. I know you'll be safe, so be smart and you'll be home for dinner." Mark says as he lets Evelyn go.

Chris tosses his gear into the back of Mark's white SUV looking eager to head out, "Alright boss I will bring her back to you." He says closing the liftgate.

"Chris, I need you to come back too, you have become like a son to me and I love you. You take care." Mark hugs Chris in a loving embrace.

Ryan joins the hug, "See, told ya." He squeezes Chris's leg a little tighter.

"Ok, enough with the lovey crap, we need to get going." Quinn crumbles the love bubble.

With a slow roll the SUV leaves down the dirt road. Now the rest of the group heads to their assigned tasks for the day. The kids head inside and out of the cold. Sarge and Angel head off to gather wood to cut, while MJ and Mark start to trade off keeping watch and chopping what wood they already had. A conversation sparks.

"So, MJ, when are you guys leaving? Are you going to leave?" Mark asks.

MJ stops his swing of the ax, "Not sure. We can't get in contact with anyone to make any kind of plan." Thwack! The ax falls.

Mark is standing closer to the water than the cabin, his back to MJ who is a few yards in front of the cabin, "What do you want to do?" Mark tries a veiled attempt to pick MJ's brain.

MJ places another log on the tree stump they use as a chopping block, "We don't get to do what we want Mark we get told what to do. That's it, even before all of this. But especially now." Thwack! More wood hits the ground.

Mark turns to look at MJ, bewilderment on his face, "What was it you did before?"

"We investigate outbreaks. Ebola in Africa, Toxic poisoning symptoms in the middle east, farmers getting a mystery flu in Montana. They need people to track that kind stuff." MJ informs him.

Full of questions, Mark goes rapid fire, "So you do what exactly? Who do you report to? For the science of it?" Mark has more but his mind is going faster than his mouth.

"Hang on there, Mark. Do you still not trust me? Even after last night?" MJ puts the ax over his shoulder and starts walking towards Mark, taking a deep breath.

In a tailspin, Mark is on the defensive, "No, that's not it." He puts out there quickly, "I Just want to know what's going on and that all seems so interesting." Mark clears up his intentions.

"Mark, I like you. We've come to kind of like all of you. You all were like a TV show we'd watch and unlike before we didn't get to turn it off and go back to camp or even have a big team of people to get other human interaction with and remove you from our minds." MJ confesses.

A shocked Mark responds, "I can understand that, but I can't help but think you aren't telling us something. Sarge is even having a hard time with it and that man never stopped loving or thinking about you."

"Really?" MJ sends a little of that shock back in Mark's direction.

Mark and MJ seem to have taken a layer of armor off now, "Yes, in fact that was probably one of the first things, real things he told me. How he'd failed with you." Mark takes a seat on the picnic table.

MJ slides up on it as well, "Of course he thinks he's failed." MJ says with an undertone of hate in his voice.

Mark, taking offense cuts him off, "NO! He doesn't think he failed because you are who you are. In his mind he failed you as his son. He hurts because you thought he wouldn't love you. He failed because he lost so much time with you. He was young when he had you and Angel, he didn't have a clue what he was doing. But from where I'm sitting you both turned out well. Two strong and smart people, both of whom seem like they care more about those they love than themselves." Mark says with anger in his voice.

MJ sits still and quiet for a few moments. Mark gets up and takes the ax and begins to chop wood, with every swing a bit of anger leaves his body. With every breath in the cold air fills his lungs and on the exhales it's like every emotion leaves in a cloud from his nose.

"Mark, I think you were my favorite to watch, you somehow had a loving relationship with everyone."

Unsure what to do with that information Mark asks, "What do you mean." He sets the ax down against the stump.

"Like I said it was like a TV show. You were always my favorite. I would watch you play with Ryan, keep an eye on Evelyn and Chris from a distance. I loved watching you and Joey interact. I could only hear your side of the conversation and never knew what he was really saying on that note pad and the little bit of signing you guys would do." MJ almost seems sad.

Mark doesn't have words to respond to what's just been said. He's frozen in a memory.

MJ Continues on with sadness in his voice, "Sometimes I would even voice him in my head. Like it was you and I talking instead." MJ now has a smile on his face.

"Why?" Mark has to ask.

"Because." MJ says.

Both men are back to being face to face, MJ still sitting at the picnic table, "Here are these two people in front of me and they are bonded. You can just tell. The US government spent a lot of time and money on teaching me how to read people and I could just tell. Even without all that training, you guys were like brothers." MJ grins with memories in his head no doubt.

"He was like a little brother. He was my best friend." Mark feels the heartbreak wash over him.

"I will never forget the day where he tried to teach you how to say, 'Sarge is an asshole' man you struggled so hard." MJ now full-on laughing.

"Oh man I remember that. He was so frustrated because I was… am so awful at signing."

Saturday August 24, 2013

It's a sunny and humid late summer afternoon in the Midwest. Ryan is losing a splash fight he started with everyone but Mark and Joey. The lake is sparkling in the sun, water warm and laughter fills the air.

Mark and Joey sit on the lake side facing each other. Joey's red hair is getting long, and the slight curl is becoming more apparent. His face looks inviting, but his eyes tell a different story.

Mark is at the point of a mental breakdown, he's been trying to learn to call Sarge an asshole, for what seems to him like years.

Joey runs through it one more time. Starting with the sign for Sarge. He brings his left hand to his mouth like he's smoking a big fat cigar. Next, he signs the letter "A" by folding his fingers down to his palm and his thumb still pointing upward and taps it to his head twice.

This is a simple thing for Joey but for whatever reason Mark keeps folding his fingers or thumb in an odd and awkward manner. Joey has tried to teach Mark the basics for a while but nothing seems to work.

Joey grabs Mark's hand and folds Mark's fingers into position and moves his hand for him. He motions to Mark to try in again.

He finally does it. Joey is at last proud of Mark. Signing 'Thank you' and rolling his eyes.

Mark, says "Sorry I'm stupid."

Joey signs, I'm sorry you're stupid too. Joey picks up the note pad and writes

I appreciate you trying to learn ASL but man you suck. I've seen kids pick it up faster than you.

Mark smiles and places his hand on Joey's shoulder, "Joey, no offense, but did you ever think it was your shitty teaching skills?"

Joey holds up his middle finger and then points it at Mark, signing. They both laugh and hug it out.

Sarge yells, "ON ME!" the group converges on Sarge who's standing knee deep in the lake. Evelyn and Elsa had just gone into Manny and Elsa's cabin.

"What is it?" Manny asks.

Sarge points to the far side of the lake, "Look, I think I saw a car."

"What, where?" Mark asks.

"There, look right there." Sarge points.

Joey is trying to track all that's going on, he takes a step closer trying to see. Chris takes a step out of his way. Now Joey is in front of everyone. Just as he notices this his head turns.

SPLASH! Sarge and Chris have pushed Joey in the lake. Splishing and splashing Joey has gotten to his feet. After he wipes the water and hair out of his face, he's met with a birthday cake. Elsa and Evelyn had brought out. Everyone is poorly but whole heartedly signing Happy Birthday to him. Even Mark.

Joey has what could be water dripping from his eyes but most likely isn't.

… WE KNOW THAT ALREADY… A voice rings in Marks ears.

December 3rd, 2013

The voice was MJ, it snaps Mark back to the cold. The world has seemed colder since losing Joey for Mark. He fights back tears, "What do you mean 'we already know that'?" Mark asks in a daze.

"I didn't say anything." MJ says confused.

Mark is tired but still sure of what he heard. Before he has time to steady his mind Ryan runs up, "Hey dad when you go out looking for wood can I come?" Ryan hops up and down.

Mark smiles and looks at MJ, "See kids used to beg to go to a candy or toy store… now they beg to go get firewood." Mark laughs.

Ryan unamused looks up into his father's eyes, "So can I, Dad?"

"That's fine son. Go get your coat and hat." Mark pushes him towards the cabin.

"Mark, can I ask you something?" MJ walks up behind him watching Ryan rush into the cabin.

"Of course."

"Were you really that bad at sign language, or was it all fake?" MJ asks intently.

"That day by the lake with Joey, you mean? No, I said I'd keep him busy while they made the cake." Mark smiles at the not-so-distant memory.

Before MJ can ask anything else Sarge and Angel return, they have a telephone pole size tree. Mark is in awe of them, "Oh my God. How the hell did you even get that?"

Angel with zero strain in her voice says, "Because Marines."

"Oorah!" Sarge cries out.

They drop the tree on the ground with a hollow thud it hits.

Mark calls Ryan outside. MJ leads the way, they set off in the opposite direction Sarge came from. The sky is still, there's very little wind. Ryan is moving a mile a minute out in front of the two men.

MJ smiles at Ryan, looking to Mark, "He's a good kid. Even with all of this he keeps his spirit intact."

"That's thanks to his mom. She did all the hard work." Mark pays homage.

They walk just a few more feet before MJ stops, "I have to know what happed to Joey? We didn't see that. All we know is he didn't return that day."

Mark doesn't stop he keeps walking through the wooded area, "He wanted to prove something, I think. All we have is who we are now."

MJ walks a step behind Mark, "I see."

Ryan interrupts MJ, "Dad, I think I hear something."

They stop and listen, growls are nearby. The three walk on, searching out the source. A small foursome of Zeeks eating what looks like a deer. MJ and Mark take action.

Before the Zeeks know what's going on they are dispatched. Nothing in comparison to the night before. The trio head back on the search for wood worth bringing back.

"Dad that was gross right?"

"Yes, it sure was Ryan."

"It made me think of that time mom made that weird raw fish stuff."

Mark laughs, pulling Ryan close.

After some more walking they find a downed tree that broke after it hit the ground. They each grab what they can carry and head back. This go round was more about scouting than gathering.

Walking up to the full tree Sarge and Angel brought back with armfuls of wood seems disappointing to Angel.

"Aww couldn't bring back anything bigger?" she jokes.

Mark doesn't laugh but he does give her a small peck on the lips. This is the first time he let his feeling drive. Angel looks him in the eyes his soul connects with hers in a new way. She can't help but pull him in for a stronger deeper kiss.

"Do you two mind?" Sarge isn't amused at all. "I mean, I know you two are a thing, but do you have to be a thing right in front of me?"

Mark takes a step back from Angel, "I'm going to go get some water." Mark stumbles over his words.

"You do that, I'd hate to have to beat you to death now that I like you again."

"SARGE!" Angel yells.

Mark, now inside getting a glass of water, overhears Manny and Elsa talking. He says something about the supplies seem like they've been taken. She responds with anger.

"Hey guys what's going on?" Mark steps in.

"Mark, I think someone has been stealing." Elsa looks up at Mark from the couch.

"Stealing? How much?"

Manny looks at the note pad, "Not much, it would have been hard to notice except after Sarge said openly he didn't trust me…"

"Manny stop just tell him." Elsa smacks him and cuts him a wifely look.

"It seems like over time enough to last one person maybe three weeks to a month."

Mark is blown away by the idea someone would do something like this. He rushes outside, straight to Sarge.

"It was you wasn't it?"

Sarge who is cutting wood stops to look at Mark, "What was me?"

"You want to go off alone, we all see it. That house you want to make yours."

Sarge pushes Mark back a little with a smile on his face, "I have no idea what you're talking about, but anything I do is for the good of this group."

Angel tries to cut the tension between the two, "What happened Mark?"

MJ takes a step back closer to Ryan. Mark looks at everyone, "Supplies have gone missing. Slowly so no one would notice."

"Hahaha." Sarge laughs a sarcastic laugh. "I'm the one who said we need to track it. Why the hell would I put my op out there to be found out?"

Mark takes up that space Sarge created with the push, "Exactly. You'd do it so you can say exactly that."

"Mark, you need to back up before I back you up." Sarge squares up to Mark.

MJ sends Ryan inside. As he gets to the door Manny opens it, he'd been watching the whole time.

"I bet it was that asshole." Sarge points at Manny.

"Don't try and blame someone else. You acted like you and I were good, you came back to be the hero."

"Mark, he wouldn't do that. I know him, that would hurt the team." Angel tries to reason with Mark.

This cuts deeply into Mark, "I should have known. You used us to get here, why would you not do it again?"

"Mark where is this coming from?" Angel is trying to reach Mark's sensibility.

"You know why Joey did what he did? Because you made him feel useless. You made him feel like you would pick him if you had to make someone bait, like he didn't bring much to the team and would be an acceptable loss."

"Now you're just talking out of your ass." Sarge takes a step back.

"Before we left that day, he asked me if I felt he was useful."

"You ever stop and think he felt like you were the problem, have you? You are God, right?"

"Sarge, lock it down, now!" Angel puts herself between the two fearing another fist fight.

"How dare you, how dare you treat it like I wasn't his friend." Mark stung by Sarge's words.

"Look Mark, I'm not sure who was stealing but no need to fight with your own." MJ speaks up.

That was enough to push Mark off the edge. Just as Mark turns to walk away still angry the supply run group pulls up. Before they get out Mark has walked off.

"Mark, Mark!" Angel cries out.

He can hear her but doesn't react at all, pulling a page from her book.

MJ runs up behind Mark, "I get you're mad but you or anyone for that matter shouldn't be out alone with this many threats around. Living and the dead.

"Fine, I'm pissed. Don't bring up Joey right now."

MJ laughs, "Whatever you say Mark, we can just walk."

That's just what they do. They walk for a while no talking just thinking. The darkness is falling early in the beginning of winter. Mark and MJ reach a road. It's not traveled as much as the road they use for the cabins but has seen use. Mark stops.

"That's weird." Mark looks both ways down this road.

"What's that?" MJ says looking at his watch.

"This road, it was mostly overgrown when we got here. I almost forgot about it." Mark kneels to look at the tire tracks.

MJ looks around, "You think it's those rednecks that attacked you the other day?"

"I don't know. It isn't on any map, but we need to go back. Now." Mark walks past MJ who's still looking around like Sarge when he sees something about to happen. "Didn't you hear…" With a thud Mark hits the ground. He can hear a car pull up. He can feel three sets of hands on his body loading him into the back. The voices are all too familiar.

"Juice him, juice him now before he comes to." Quinn voice fades.

The world goes black.

Have you ever woken up from a dream, and it felt so real not because it was what you wanted but what you've already lived?

I feel cold, cold and wet. As I look around the room its dark except a spotlight shining down on me. My arms and legs are tied to the chair I'm in. I yell out "Hey! Can anybody hear me?"

I can't see if the is door behind me just the concrete walls. The cold creeps into my toes and I realize I don't have shoes or socks on.

Hopping in my chair trying to turn around. CRASH! I hit the ground.

A door opens, I'm filled with fear. I'm frozen with it. "Who's there?"

"See I told you he was awake." Quinn's voice comes from behind me.

"Get him up." MJ commands.

As my chair is lifted, I see MJ, Quinn and Dallas in the room now a file on a desk, "What's going on? What are you doing?" UMFF! Dallas punches me in the stomach.

"Enough, Dallas, he's told us all he knows. It was long and mostly pointless, but it was every-thing-he-knows." MJ says with a song like cadence.

"What are you doing?" I ask again.

"Mark, I'm sorry about this. Truly I am. We need someone, someone that could vanish if this doesn't work." MJ takes a seat on the table. His voice sounds friendly, but I don't trust the look in his eye.

"Mark, you have been chosen by the US government. Chosen to be one of the first in the human trials!" Quinn rejoices.

My ears are ringing but I think I heard her right, "Trial for what?"

Dallas slaps me in the back of my head, I cut him a look because if I wasn't in the chair, he'd be surprised what he gets. Quinn walks up and squats down to eye level, "Mark you didn't think anyone was working on a treatment, did you?"

"Yes Mark, we were tasked with finding John Doe and a few others to run a human trial on. Now our secret is out." MJ puts his hands on his cheeks.

I try my best Sarge impression, "Hahaha," I laugh, "Did it work?"

Dallas smacks me again, "We haven't given it to you yet fuck face. I wish you'd have just let me kill him at that hotel like we planned." Dallas looks at MJ disappointment on his face.

All I can think is how bad he smells, it's like B.O. mixed with something that died. He walks over to the table. I thank him for removing his stench from near me.

"Hey, no need for you to get any more hurt Mark be nice." MJ says.

I am unsure what will happen to me but my need to know what's going on is far too great, "If you were going to kill me a few weeks ago why am I here now?"

MJ jumps up, "That's the big question isn't it? Why you? Well we'd agreed on Joey but the day at the hotel, we were ready to grab him on your way back to your cozy cabin. Only he didn't come back."

My heart sinks, "Why Joey?"

"If you can't tell we don't like when our lab rats talk back." MJ says turning around facing the door. Dallas starts to make rat noises and faces at me.

"You are all insane."

Quinn flips open the folder dramatically, "No, we are not. We have been entrusted with the fate of mankind!"

No, these people are insane. The look in her eyes is 100% crazy. MJ is talking like the bad guy in a spy movie and Dallas is making me feel like he would eat my liver. They are all crazy.

MJ walks over to me his boots clicking on the floor, "Get one thing straight, you are our second choice. We can make a third or fourth or hell even a fifth."

I can see the same look in his eyes that Sarge has only this one seems to have less regard for life. "Where are my kids and my friends?"

"They are probably searching the woods for you. That or those rednecks killed them." Dallas chimes in.

"Mark we can do this the hard way or the easy way, it really is up to you." MJ calms down.

"Fine what do you need me to do?" I give in because I know I can't fight my way out of this chair, but if they move me, I may have a chance.

"Thank you, Mark. Your country is grateful for your sacrifice. They wanted it to be a choice, but we don't much care one way or the other." Quinn mutters.

"What do I have to do?" my pulse quickens.

"Well Mark..." Alarms start to go off before MJ finishes his sentence. They leave the room in a hurry. I'm back to trying to get out of this chair. I swear this chair is way stronger than any that Sarge has been tied to.

Think, Mark what can get you out of here. As I scan the room to see what I can use to get out, Quinn runs back into the room, she draws her knife.

"Mark run we had a lab breach you have to run." She cuts my right hand out of the strap, "Take this, down the hall to the right are clothes and supplies." I wonder why now she cares if I live or die. No matter because I'm free.

She runs back out of the room. I can hear her scream. I'm probably not going to lose any sleep over that, however. I manage to get my left hand free, not a moment too soon. A Zeek finds its way into the room.

"Thanks Quinn, couldn't have closed the door on your way out?"

Ok now for the elephant in the room. I sit in wait for the Zeek to get close before knifing it in the head. Its blood is warm on my cold wet skin. I quickly undo my leg restraints. I peek around the corner, bloody drag marks lead down the hall to the left. She said right so that's a good sign already.

I find the room she was talking about. On a shelf in the small concrete room are my clothes not a random set but mine from a drawer in my cabin. Under that is a water-tight box. I open it again to my surprise it's my backpack that I use when I go out to do a run.

I open the bag, inside are the supplies Manny was telling us were missing. I find the stupid croquet handle.

"Why the hell did they bring this thing?"

I suddenly realize that I blew up at Sarge for nothing, it was all them. They played me into this. Forced it to happen.

I don't have the time to stay and think about how I messed up. I need to move. As I run down the hall every time my feet hit the ground even in shoes the numb feeling makes the next step hurt more. This place looks like an underground bunker. *How long was I down here?* I think.

I find an emergency exit. As I push the door open, I let the fear fill me not knowing what's on the other side. I don't let the fear control me but let it fuel me.

The door opens with a howl, wind and snow fly in like a blizzard. I step out and I see mountains and no lights of any kind. It's dark maybe not late night but past early evening, the cold and wind almost knock me over.

"WHERE THE FUCK AM I?"

For more information on the Here We Remain series check out our social media.

Here After

Book III coming soon!

writerhereweremain.blogspot.com

HEREWEREMAIN2018

Special Thanks to:

Kelly Jonson

Faye Homes

www.ingramcontent.com/pod-product-compliance
Lightning Source LLC
Chambersburg PA
CBHW071940150726
47999CB00001B/273